Penguin Science Fiction
In Solitary

Evacuated from London during the bombing, Garry
Kilworth's mother produced him in York in 1941. His
parents were travellers, and his teenage years were
spent in Southern Arabia, which in the fifties had an
exciting and friendly atmosphere.

After two years at an Air Force technical college, he
was sent to the Far East to immerse himself in the
heady orientalism of Malaya and Singapore. He also
spent a year drifting on a tiny coral island in the
Maldives of the Indian Ocean, which resulted in heavy
reading and skin diving—for light relief he boxed
featherweight in the Far East Air Force championships.

Later years saw Garry Kilworth enjoying prolonged
periods in Germany, Africa, Bahrain, Aden, Malta and
Cyprus. It was during those years that he began to
write fiction and poetry, and in 1974 he won the
Gollancz/*Sunday Times* Science Fiction competition.

He is now a Senior Telecommunications Executive
with a communications firm that operates on a
world-wide basis. Apart from delving into new
communications' developments and writing his heart
out, he enjoys the family activities of canoeing,
camping in the wilds, ornithology and collecting
anything useless to nature or Man. He is married to a
bookdealing schoolteacher and they have two teenage
children.

Garry Kilworth's second novel, *The Night of Kadar*,
is forthcoming in Penguins.

Garry Kilworth

In Solitary

Penguin Books

Penguin Books Ltd, Harmondsworth,
Middlesex, England
Penguin Books, 625 Madison Avenue,
New York, New York 10022, U.S.A.
Penguin Books Australia Ltd, Ringwood
Victoria, Australia
Penguin Books Canada Ltd, 2801 John Street,
Markham, Ontario, Canada L3R 1B4
Penguin Books (N.Z.) Ltd, 182–190 Wairau Road,
Auckland 10, New Zealand

First published by Faber and Faber Ltd, 1977
Published in Penguin Books 1979

With acknowledgements to the article 'Isles of the
Pacific' by Kenneth P. Emory, PLD (*National
Geographic*, December 1974), for aspects of
Polynesian navigation used in this novel

Made and printed in Great Britain by
Richard Clay (The Chaucer Press) Ltd,
Bungay, Suffolk
Set in Linotype Pilgrim

For Chantelle, Richard and Annette,
who already read me too well

      ... but there's no cage to him

more than to the visionary his cell:
his stride is wildernesses of freedom:
the world rolls under the long thrust of his heel.
Over the cage floor the horizons come.

TED HUGHES, *The Jaguar*

The Soal Law

1. No member of the Human Race, born a native of the Planet Earth, may have contact with any other such native, by any medium, natural or otherwise, after the age of 170 months, except for the performance of mating.

2. No member of the Human Race under 170 months of age, born a native of the Planet Earth, may have contact with any male member of the same race.
The penalty for disobedience of the Soal Law is death.

I

From the Sennish of the Weyym:
... and the sun shall inhale ...

Mating

Tangiia was building his mating canoe. It was a Satawal, narrow and sleek with a slim outrigger for stability, for in the mating waters speed would be essential. It might mean the difference between a joyous union with a beautiful female, or violent death in the hands of a rival.

This was to be Tangiia's third mating since the age of one hundred and eighty, for copulation with the Polynesian females was permitted only once every thirty-five months – a mandatory restriction imposed since the Soal first consolidated their victory over Earth exactly $70^2 + 83$ months previously.

The young man smoothed the bark with a piece of sandstone, running his free hand lovingly over the wood. He already had his fishing canoe, but that was outriggerless and purpose built. It needed too much draught for the sport of mating, being constructed to hold a bellyful of fish. The craft he needed now would be as light as a seabird, and would skim across the surface of the water hardly touching the waves along its arrow-straight course. That would be in the escape from the mêlée. During the capture, he would need to tack in and out of other boats and then run a female down. The seamanship of the females was as good as that of their male counterparts – sometimes better, because of their lithe movements, their spry bodies.

Tangiia remembered his first female as he sat working under the sun on the sugar-white sands of his small island. She had been brown and salty – and very experienced. Without Tangiia realizing she had drawn his attention and led him from the pack.

At first he had been disappointed – a young man likes an equally young woman with whom to share his prolonged lust – but he later understood that his lack of sexual knowledge would have left both partners not only disappointed, but prematurely exhausted. Although the first union with Keha had been a savage, clawing match, not without bloodletting on both sides, the controlled coaxing in the later movements, over the allowed five days, aroused him again and again to the performance of the act.

Keha had been small and agile, with bright, eager eyes: a woman of some 312 months. She had long nails which gave Tangiia some considerably painful but delightful moments at the dagger-point of ecstasy. He had enjoyed everything with her and did not want to exchange her, as was the custom, after the first two days. However, his ideas had not been shared by her, nor by the other man. There had been a fight in which his *lei o mano* had found the throat of his opponent, tearing an ugly wound in the man's flesh.

This was the way of things. Occasionally fewer men returned from the mating than male children were born. The Soal had planned it so.

A bird floated overhead and Tangiia shouted and waved his fist at it.

'Foul treader of wind, leave me.'

Birds had fallen into disrepute since the arrival of the conquering Soal, for the invaders resembled birds themselves, with pointed beak-like faces and a web of elastic skin joining the upper and lower limbs. They were approximately a metre tall – two thirds the height of an Earthman – and, to speak truthfully, were more like flying foxes than birds, but fine hair-like feathers covered their bodies. The feathers greyed with age, like hair, and gave the elderly Soal a ghostly, awful presence. Birds like gulls therefore, with white feathers, were especially despised by humans.

'Go, go,' shouted Tangiia, and picked up a stone from the beach ready to hurl it at the bird if it had the audacity to land within range.

It eyed the Polynesian warily, and then wheeled away on a warm current of air towards the sun.

'He goes,' said Tangiia, addressing his boat and waving his arm contemptuously in the direction of the departing bird. Tangiia often spoke to his boat, as he spoke to the fish, and the wind, the trees and the rocks – and Tangiia was not mad. Man liked society and under the Soal his companions, apart from pets, were inanimate.

The last time Tangiia had mated, he had searched the temporarily white-scarred sea, covered with knifing craft, for Keha. For three years he had thought of nothing but Keha. She had visited his mind during the wild storms when he lay shivering with cold and fright and he had used the images of their threshings in the strapped-together canoes to chase away the demons from his mind. She had lain with him, in spirit, on the hot sands during the days when the sun draws the water from the seas and fills the air with its weight.

On the second voyage to the mating waters, held in the south of Oceania, the area surrounding north-eastern Ostraylea, Tangiia had dreamed of his woman. He followed a *kaveinga*, a star path, south-west towards his goal, watching the horizon during the night for one star after another to appear as a line to navigate by. When one star was too high, another rose to take its place on the horizon, and so on, until morning. Polynesians had been navigating thus for many thousands of months, using the deep ocean swells, imperceptible to a novice, to nudge the way during the day, and following the *kaveinga* during the dark hours. Polynesian navigators use no charts, no compasses, no instruments of man. They employ their senses and the natural ways of the universe: the star paths, the *panakenga* stars lying low on the horizon, the swells, currents, the direction of the flight of birds and the fascinating *te lapa*: underwater streaks of light that flash beneath the surface and point the way to the islands, said to have their origins in volcanic disturbances.

'I am coming for you,' Tangiia had called over the waves as he raced the dolphins towards Ostraylea.

'I am coming for your brown body, you witch of seas. I come to taste the salt of your skin again, and kiss drops of water from your brows.'

He had called delightedly in the language of the Terrans: a language that had covered the globe before the Soal arrived and separated all men from their brothers. It was the language taught him by his mother, until she left him, as was the Soal Law, at the age of one hundred and seventy, to be ever alone until death. Except, of course, for the brief periods of mating that were like bright jewels embedded in the blankness of his life.

Only a few of the Old Polynesian words remained: among those, the sacred words of the navigators that were prized for their inherent beauty.

Nearing Ostraylea, Tangiia had found himself in the midst of many other canoes and he gripped a shark-toothed *lei o mano*, relic of his ancestors, in one hand as he steered his canoe with the other. It was a time of great personal danger and he had been determined to have his Keha, if he was to die in the attempt.

The sails of the women's mating canoes were seen coming from the east and a great moan of unlocked desire swept over the water as the thousands of small craft converged upon one another.

Tangiia's eyes had been everywhere, anxiously searching, searching, for the bright blue sail of his lover. But there were many blue sails – and he never found Keha. After skimming past a dozen canoes he had finally struck a wave-skipping craft amidships in the crowded waters, had pitched forward and had landed at the feet of a beautiful, damp-eyed girl. She tore the cloth from his loins and soon he forgot his longing for Keha – her memory was lost in an explosion of athletic passion. If Keha had been an eager, blazing fire, Peloa was a volcano: a small, slim arc of thrusting lava-hot flesh with small conical breasts that burned their points into his own body.

Behind them, Ostraylea stood, the dark ring where the old waterline had once been, stark against the turquoise oceanic backdrop.

Behind that was one of the great mushroom towers. Around the mushroom tower high in the air, rolled a sky wheel – a transport of the Soal. It was inspecting its charge, apparently oblivious to the animalistic behaviour going on in the seas below it.

Suddenly it had paused, and then rolled closer to a leglike strut. It had seen something worth reporting – a fissure, like a lightning crack, upon the shell of the tower, which appeared to be spreading. It was the cause of immediate and grave concern, and the wheel's pilot contacted his base. Cracks were continually appearing on the Ostraylean tower. The day would come when it would need to be reinforced by more than minor repairs.

2

... its worlds slowly: the drawing in of a gentle breath ...

Banishment

I faced the master, Klees of Brytan, as he trembled with rage. A wave ran through his feathers like the wind over a field of long grass – a sign that I was truly in disgrace and that death should not be an unexpected punishment this time.

We were in the Hall of Weyym, a religious sect of the Soal. The Klees was sitting crosslegged and I, standing beneath his high stool, was looking up at him. It was daylight outside the Hall, and the sun angled through the mosaic of the chipped-crystal walls. However, the thermostats kept the room temperature constant. On a smaller stool some two metres high, beside his father, sat my friend Lintar. He was regarding me with hurt and puzzled eyes.

The diamond mouth of the Klees opened and he grunted in the thick accents of a Soal speaking Terran, punctuating each word with a breath.

'You have betrayed us. After all our kindness you have finally shown us your true side, Terran animal. You have also betrayed your own father, who was a good and obedient servant, now in the arms of the Universal Weyym. I must contemplate your punishment.' His head went down between his prominent clavicles: the classical Soal pose of concentration I called *stool*, owing to the piece of furniture upon which they usually did their thinking.

I thought about my father, a poor weak man; eager to please and happy to remain alive. If serving the Soal meant freedom from the fear of death or banishment, then my father would be the first to proclaim his submission. They killed him when I reached 170 months of age. I did not despise him: he had been my father, and in that role had been a kind and good man. But I could no more be like him than a fish can be a bird – not for an hour, not for a second. Consequently I grew to manhood sullen and obstinate, with only one friend in the world, the Klees's own son. Had we not been close, I should have died much sooner, by Endrod's hand.

'You must go,' cried the Klees finally.

'Father . . .' began Lintar. But the Klees silenced his intervention with a quick wave of his arm.

'Not this time my son. We have been lenient too often and for too long. Any mercy shown might jeopardize my own political career – Endrod would have the human dead. As it is I must face him with a considerably lighter award of punishment than he expects.' Endrod was the Chief Librarian and my greatest tormentor.

The Klees turned to glare at me.

'You have three hours,' he stated, 'you understand?'

I nodded. All the conversation between father and son had taken place in Soal, a language spoken at a frequency high above the audio range of the human ear, but I was adept at mouth reading and knew what had passed between them.

Then he stretched out his arms and legs and glided over my head towards the entrance, not looking down. I was banished from Brytan – a light sentence when you consider that I had been discovered investigating the tapes contained in the Soal history archives.

His father having now left us, Lintar began to question me in that sorrowful voice of his. He was a spoilt and rather selfish young Soal, but I was his property and when a youth's favourite companion is taken from him he feels it is the most tragic moment of his life.

'Why did you do it, Cave? What were you looking for that was so important to you?'

I hung my head as if in shame. From the suppressed frustration in his tone I knew he was only a whisper away from striking me and I had no wish to leave this land with more enemies than I had already. Endrod alone was enough for any man.

'Shall we walk the vats?' I said. This was an attempt at placating him.

Lintar's feathers rose, and then slowly fell, and I knew he had taken command of himself once more. He was nearing adulthood and his petulant outbursts of temper were becoming less frequent. It was a pity I had now disgraced myself, for it was reasonably certain that Lintar would attain the position his father held – he was competent in the affairs of state and his education had been channelled to that end. As his companion I would have been in an enviable position – for a human. There were few of us enough as it was, on dry land. Soon I was to join the unlucky ones – out on the mud.

On the vat walks the air was pleasant enough. It was, as always, full of the aerobic bacteria on which the Soal fed. I am told humans do not benefit from the odours that are exuded from the breeding sludge in the oblong vats, as the Soal do, but it was difficult to believe because the stench was so enjoyable. As a human I ate solid foods, though I drank liquids like the Soal. There again was another difference in our biological make-up. The Soal waited until their liquids turned sour before drinking them – I had tried that as a boy, and had made myself extremely ill. Lintar used to enjoy watching my efforts at mimicking his natural habits, until his father warned him that copying the Soal might end in my death by poisoning.

'Is there anything you want me to do for you before you go?' questioned Lintar.

We were walking on one of the broad rectangular paths that formed the walls to the vats. The smell was delicious and I breathed deeply. Then I answered.

'I wondered,' I said, stepping aside for two Soal that walked directly towards me, 'whether I might be allowed to take a crossbow with me? I have heard that the mud flats can be dangerous – the humans that live out there are untrained and vicious.' I looked down on Lintar's face. It was a large request. The responsibility would be his, should any Soal be attacked with the weapon. His lidless eyes looked upwards and studied my own features.

'But the humans must obey the laws of the Soal. Why should they want to kill one another?'

'I have heard there are many, and that territories are jealously guarded. If I should happen to stray accidentally into another man's or woman's area, or find it necessary to do so because of lack of food, then I would need a weapon.'

This was a lie and Lintar probably knew it, but he realized that I should have a hard time taking care of myself. I had never been alone before.

Lintar struggled with himself inwardly. There was a sensible course to take, and then there was the indulgence of a childhood companion whose need was desperate. Finally, and predictably for Lintar, he chose the latter.

'You shall have your crossbow,' he grunted, aware that he was being foolish. 'Just take care you only use it in an emergency.'

I snorted. 'What do you care for other humans?'

'Nothing,' he replied quickly. 'Let no more be said. I shall obtain the crossbow for you, but if you are caught with it I trust you to keep my name inside you to the death.'

I nodded, and then changed the subject, leaning over the rails to a vat and pointing into the sludge. I thought about death, a subject which I find infinitely interesting and contemplate for long hours. It is the last great mystery. Soal speak of death as a fact but rarely wonder on the after effects of the termination of their own lives. The Universal Weyym is a god of life, not death. Death is a vacuum and is the same word in the Soal language as 'Zero'. 'When I reach zero,' they say. They count the months of their lives backwards, beginning at one thousand and fifty. They never count below one. Some elderly Soal have been *one* for as long as I can remember. Each extra month they stay alive is a renewed 'one'.

'This is the vat which claimed the life of Askreenata – do you remember? She tried to glide the length of it and the breeze dropped? What a way to die – to drown in ...'

'That's enough,' snapped Lintar sharply. 'Enough talk of death. You are a morbid human. Why death fascinates you so much I cannot imagine. It is dwelling on nothing, for that is death, nothingness.'

We finished our walk back at the church and the Klees was waiting for me with a knapsack of food. Lintar slipped away, I hoped to fetch the promised crossbow. Then I was led through the accommodation area to the sea wall.

Beyond the sea wall, between the continent of Hess and Brytan stretched kilometres of tideland which was covered, in some places by only a few centimetres of water, at high tide. Once upon a time there had been a permanent channel of water between Brytan and Hess which made Brytan a full-time island. The earthquake of 2083 Old Time had changed the physical relationships between Brytan and Yurop, as Hess was called in those times. As well as the structural changes in the substrata of the western shores of Hess, the Soal had constructed great tidal gates, which also served them as a bridge, between the south-east tip of Brytan and the Hessian peninsula. Thus they were able to control the depth of the tideway to a certain degree and prevent flooding during the spring tides.

I had now to go out and live on the mud wastes, never again to set foot on the dry land of my home country. I was the last human to leave Brytan and I went regretfully. The Soal had all the main land over the whole Earth. Some of them, the central continentals, had never seen a human in their whole lives, yet once upon a time we crawled over the surface of the world in our millions. Now we lived on the islands and areas of waste ground which the Soal did not want. A race of hermits that prayed to the Weyym of Boundless Space for the simultaneous death of every living Soal in the universe.

3

... and the subsurface Soal will quit their stark
passages ...

Needles

Mudflats must be the most depressing of all the landscape scenes
to fall on the human eye. The only marks a person can leave on
that desert of sludge are footprints, and even those are transient
– they remain for the length of time between two high tides.
Then the world is wiped smooth and clean of a mud dweller's
only solid proof that he is not a ghost. Nothing is made, nothing is created on the mud. People are there to exist only – not
to build histories for the conjecture of others. When the last
body, be it a thousand years hence, has rotted away, the mud
will hold no secrets. All artifacts owned by mud dwellers bear
the marks of Soal manufacture, and the human bones will be
taken away with the tide.

Mud dwellers live only for a few hours at a time. They disappear with each oncoming tide, into one of the transparent
needle towers, thinner and taller than minarets, that spike the
mud, while the sea washes away the patterns of their existence.

I was prodded from behind and realized I had been standing
for a few minutes regarding the grey wastes. I was beginning to
wonder what in Weyym's mind had induced me to go foraging
through the Tape Library. Curiosity? Rebellion? Stupidity? The
Klees would say the latter. Now I was doomed to spend the rest
of my life, probably a very short one, up to my eyebrows in filth.

The Klees pushed some mudshoes into my hands just as
Lintar came running towards us with a blanket, which he
quickly bundled into my arms. I took it gratefully, feeling the
hardness of the weapon within its folds.

'Thank you Lintar,' I said quietly.

He nodded. 'In case you get wet,' he said in that peculiar shrill accent. For all the hours in the day the mushroom towers kept the temperature of the atmosphere fairly constant, at a comfortable heat. Lintar had once told me that if the mushroom towers ever cease to function the Earth would become uninhabitable for the Soal. He did not say for how long they could live in varying temperatures, but I understood it to be a very short time.

The two Soal, the old one and his young son, stood watching my naked form as I walked through the gates. It seemed to me that they were the sad ones, these two pigmy-sized aliens, and I the lucky one, setting forth on a fantastic adventure. I waved, but they had never understood the significance of that particular gesture – my father had used it just before the executioner twisted the switch that reduced him to dust – and they had merely stood, as now, with folded arms, looking vaguely helpless. How had creatures like these conquered the world?

Once outside the great sea wall I began walking, and after a few metres of hard soil I was on the mud. I pulled on the tear-shaped mudshoes and plodded forward, with no other plan in mind than to make for a needle tower, for the high tide was only three hours away. Perhaps in a few months I could return and find Endrod's wrath abated? If I lived that long.

Endrod was the one Soal that had pressed for my father's execution. The Librarian had had an enmity towards my father. The other seven Soal on the Circle would have turned a blind eye to the Soal Law concerning Humans, but Endrod forced them into opening both eyes. The bat-like flapping of his arms during oratory had impressed even me – and I had not been able to hear the words he was speaking.

During the months my father had worked for the Klees he had stumbled innocently on a secret and, somehow, it had involved Endrod. It had been Endrod that had received the punishment from the Soal Circle and he was demoted to the position of Librarian. What post he held before that I did not know – but I had the feeling that therein lay the key to the whole affair.

Since that time (I was then only twelve months old), Endrod had extended himself in destroying humans, especially trained ones, and his principal targets had been my father and myself. Now he had beaten both of us and as far as I knew there was only one other human on dry land – the elderly companion of the Klees of Far Enlich, west of Brytan. It was certain that I had never seen one.

I pulled the lightweight crossbow from the blanket and inspected it. It was an exquisitely made object, wrought from a black metal new to Earth and brought by the Soal. However, the design of the instrument was indigenous and merely one of those things the aliens had inexplicably latched on to when they looted our old cities. They had scorned ninety-eight per cent of our innovations and technology, and had thrown all their enthusiasm into the other two per cent, which consisted of articles that followed no logical pattern in themselves and were separated by dates of discovery or invention over thousands of months. The loom, the glass bottle, the crossbow and the smell of lemons were but four that I knew of – there were others, but as for their connections there seemed to be none. They were objects picked by a blind finger running down an inventory and even I, who had lived two hundred and forty months amongst the Soal, had no sensible explanation to offer.

There were four bolts clipped to the stock of the bow – two to each side. I unclipped one and fitted it to the discharge channel, but resisted the urge to wind the mechanism: I did not want a bolt accidentally loosing itself into my foot.

The mudflats were endless, and twice I caught sight of humans. Both times I stopped and waited until they were at a safe distance before continuing. I had a vague plan in mind to cross the flats to the land I knew lay on the other side. Yurop, which the Soal called Hess. It was much larger than Brytan, and in places the mountains reached high up into the clouds. It was big enough to enable a human to live without being disturbed by Soal or others of his own kind.

Suddenly I sank up to my knees in a particularly soft patch of the grey-black sludge. It had begun to drizzle with rain from above the temperature controlled zone. I wrenched a foot clear, but left a mudshoe beneath the mire and had to reach an arm's length down into it to retrieve the shoe. The other foot came up more easily. As long as I took it slowly the sucking action of the mud was not powerful enough to hinder my progress.

However, I was now covered in filth and the rain was becoming heavier by the minute. I began to feel very, very miserable. Suddenly there was a new danger. If the rain became too dense, I should not be able to see the needle towers and the first flood of water from the incoming tide would slow my progress.

I picked out a tower through the drizzle and began to quicken my steps towards it, but it was slow and difficult work across the sludge. I tried to remember certain points Lintar had mentioned on our walk; if you begin to sink in deep mud, do not struggle; lie flat and stretch out all four limbs. How he knew the correct procedure in deep mud was conjectural. I doubted he had ever been beyond the sea wall on foot, although I knew that he had been hunting sea birds with a crossbow from a mudskate vehicle. Perhaps the Soal learned a few safety rules before embarking on an expedition?

The black ooze crept up my body by degrees and the shoes flicked dollops of the stuff up my back and into my long hair. I trudged on for the next two hours while dusk came down, realizing, all too late, that I had left an easy, soft life behind me. My bungled attempt to find some incriminating evidence with which to enact revenge on Endrod had been a poor failure, and the reverse of what I hoped to achieve had come about: I was the one who had been banished.

Night was coming on and I had only a few minutes in which to find the tower. It had been directly ahead. Perhaps I had missed it? I turned and looked through the rain, which was running in rivulets down my face, neck and chest. It was silt-laden and uncomfortable. No tower. I stumbled on, and then, suddenly there it was, almost at my nose. I grabbed the inset rungs of the ladder and began to climb: I still had to get to a segment and the first was several metres above my head. I hoped I could find a segment with no other human inside.

I had gone barely a metre when the water began swilling around the base of the needle. It was now a race against the tide. With the blanket containing the crossbow tied sling-fashion over one shoulder I began to climb for my life – and the water rose with every scrambling step. It whirled with angry white-flecked mouths below me. I had visions of disappearing down one of the throats of eddying foam.

With my arms aching and my chest heaving I made the first ledge and entered the segment gasping and pulling on the air with my lungs. It was dark in the segment and I lay on the cold floor and cherished my agony, listening to the waves throwing shoulders at the flexible, swaying tower.

Over the next few days I made my way from needle to needle, the soiling of my belaboured body becoming a continuing process, for although I could wash in the tower there was nothing to shift the obstinate patches.

I carefully avoided any humans I saw, of course. I had no desire to be caught breaking the one law for which there was no reprieve from death, no matter who or what one's friends were. The far coast was reached but the sea wall was as high and as well guarded as the one I had left. There was to be no escape in that direction.

My rations had run out and I was now living on shellfish grubbed from the mud. Hair had grown over my face, I was constantly hungry and exhausted and I began to view the world with a hard and bitter eye. After my visit to the Hessian wall I was determined to obtain a full night's rest and I climbed the nearest needle, curled up in a corner of a segment and fell instantly asleep.

It was still dark when I awoke and nagging pains in my stomach called for food. As I reached for my shoulder bag a soft moan came from the corner of the segment farthest from me. I froze, thinking I had misheard, and that the noise had its origins outside the tower. The wind, or the sea, if it was still high.

I convinced myself that this was the case, and once again reached out for the bag. A shrill scream tore through the stillness of the room and every nerve in my body sent needles of fear to my brain.

4

... venturing outwards towards the spiral of my eye ...

Stella

After the scream had subsided there was the sound of heavy breathing from the far corner of the segment, punctuated by quick, sharp sobs. Grabbing my crossbow I wound the mechanism and pointed the instrument into the darkness.

'Who's that?' I whispered gruffly. 'I have a weapon.'

The moans and sobs continued but no answer was forthcoming.

'Answer quickly or I may have to kill you,' I said louder, not sure in myself whether I really would have the courage to release the bolt.

'I'm ... I'm Stella,' came a laboured reply. Then a whimper and another long brain-screwing scream.

'A human?' I snapped, alert to danger.

'Yes, like yourself. I saw you asleep and I hoped I would not have to disturb you, but I'm afraid ...'

'So am I, so am I, if we're caught,' I gabbled, 'we'll both be put to death. No mistake about that. You'll have to leave – and quickly.'

'Not me,' she part-laughed and part-moaned, as if there was an enormous joke hovering in the air somewhere, if only one of us had the humour to catch it.

'Are you wounded? Why are you crying?'

'I'm in pain,' said the small, feminine voice, which for some reason awakened solicitous feelings in my breast. I actually felt sympathy towards this human being that was threatening my existence with her presence.

'Then I'll have to go,' I said at length. It seemed reasonable.

If she were ill she had to have somewhere to stay, away from the mud.

She screamed long and loud again and then her breath came out hissingly.

'Please stay,' she cried, 'I'm having a baby. I'm afraid.'

'You're afraid, you're afraid?' I yelled again in a panic. 'I don't know anything about babies but I know we'll both be executed ...'

Suddenly her voice became hard.

'Don't be such a coward. Stay and keep a woman company while she gives birth to human life.'

This sentence hit me, full force, in a part of me I never knew existed.

I put down the crossbow feeling tremendously guilty – as though I had just broken a Soal Law, which of course was exactly what I was doing. I went across the floor and felt around, touching something soft, moist and warm.

'Not there,' she said sharply. 'Here. Just hold my hand. It'll all be over with soon.'

It was not 'over with' soon. It took four hours, and by that time the dawn had arrived and I found myself clutching the hand of a naked angular-faced human woman with bright blue eyes and long, exceptionally dirty red hair. Stella. My first real human contact apart from family. Both of us were covered in sweat and the new baby was laid in the blanket.

There was plenty of fresh water to be had in the needle and I washed the infant where it lay – beyond that I had no knowledge of what to do. A cord hung from inside of the mother and I wondered whether this ought to be severed.

'Leave it,' said Stella, when I asked. 'I'll deal with it.'

So I went out, and down the ladder to fetch food. I tried, unsuccessfully, to pin a seabird with the crossbow, but only managed to lose a valuable bolt in the deep mud. I made do with shellfish, and took several handfuls back to her. She seemed grateful. While we were eating, an appalling thought came to me.

'How did you come to be having a baby?' I uttered, rather ridiculously. 'Now, I mean.'

She smiled ruefully. 'You mean the mating period is not for

a while yet? Don't be a fool. Where have you been living all your life?'

'Among the Soal,' I replied without a thought.

'What?' She sat up sharply from where she had been lying; her full breasts bounced heavily on her chest and I put out my hands instinctively to stop them quivering. She knocked my hands away roughly, glaring at my audacity.

'You're a spy,' she snarled, the bottom lip curling.

'No, no. Not at all. I've been banished. I did something wrong you see. They sent me away.'

'Oh.' She lay back. 'I thought for a moment ... but never mind.'

She smiled at me now and I felt warm all over my face.

'You seem nice enough,' she said. 'I don't want to cause you trouble. You'd better leave us now.' She beamed at the infant beside her which had been trying to penetrate our eardrums for some considerable time.

'Does a baby ever stop crying?' I asked, to change the subject.

Stella laughed and the segment filled with our intimacy. It was a feeling I had never known before and at the time seemed quite worth dying for.

'Not often,' she choked. 'Here give her to me.'

I gingerly picked up the 'her' – a fact I had not noticed before and watched Stella stifle the cries with one of her breasts. Soon the baby was happily feeding and we were able to continue our conversation.

I told Stella practically my life's story in an hour. Hers took longer, and was one of such hardship and privation I wondered how she could still find it in herself to laugh. She was, she thought, somewhere between two hundred and two hundred and fifty months old and had been born in a needle, of a mud-mother such as herself. However, her mother had been a virtuous woman and only copulated in the mating period. She looked after her daughter until the age of 120 months, when she was attacked by a band of human males during a night in a needle. When they had finished sating themselves they disposed of her. Thereafter Stella watched and fended for herself. Soal hunting parties, she said, could be extremely generous. And even the Soal Military had been known to hand out scraps of food. Mostly the military were dreaded, for contrary to my understanding, clandestine meetings between humans were frequent out on the mud. It occurred to me that the Klees would be horrified if he ever learned of the lightness in which the laws were taken despite Soal. Their rule was not only divide and conquer, but keep divided and keep conquered. Humans were vicious animals that hunted in packs and the only way to keep them civilized was to keep them apart. Until the Soal had arrived we were on the road to self-destruction: the aliens were our salvation.

I intended to stay with Stella only until she was fit enough to travel but when it became time for me to leave I put it off – and kept putting it off, and eventually we both realized that we would rather be together and risk being caught, than part company. Stella was more reluctant than I was to remain as a unit. It was not out of regard or fear for the law that she was unenthusiastic about remaining together. She was not as afraid of discovery as I was. Perhaps she did not like me as much as I did her and the child? Whatever her reasons, she was certainly not unkind to me, and I was grateful for that. I was very inexperienced in the ways of my new world and she could have managed as well without me. You could say I was an encumbrance for the first few weeks but I learned many things. I learned that the Soal handed out traps for catching fish and the larger types of shellfish, like lobsters, from time to time. This generosity was irregular and very occasional, so those that did own traps were extremely possessive over them. I learned that much could be done with seaweed to make a change from fish, and that rock pools were a source of small delicacies such as shrimps.

I myself discovered certain pieces of conjectural information. For instance I strongly suspected that vitamins were added to our water supply.

'If you don't drink the tower water you become ill,' Stella informed me. I was curious as to the symptoms.

'What kind of ill?' I asked.

'Different kinds.'

That was all I could get out of her on this subject. I believe she was afraid to speak of illnesses – they were nameless dreads that haunted her waking hours. She had no doubt seen many people die. There was other water to drink, that flowed onto the mud from rivers but I could not account for the Soal open-handedness. Why did they not let us all die?

We managed to avoid other humans on our travels. There were many of the crystal needle towers and few of us. The Soal Military were another matter. They would pick up a human on the slightest provocation – probably to keep our numbers low. In the first six weeks we had two brushes with them but since we were wise enough to sleep in separate segments in the needles, we were not caught together.

The Soal travelled over the mud in flying vehicles and could check segments of the transparent towers visibly, day or night. However, they rarely came at night. When they did, they would hover around outside the tower after lighting it internally with some form of remote switching, checking each segment carefully. Consequently those in the towers further abroad were forewarned of the Soal approach.

Stella was always brusque with the Soal – she had the facility of being able to bait them without going far enough for them to become angered. A lifetime's learning put to practice.

She also had the uncanny knack, or skill, of knowing the approximate time – even at night and during a cloudy day. A necessary attribute where one's life depended upon accuracy of the clock within an hour.

The mud wastes, smooth and ugly; the monotony broken only by wrinkles, ridges and rays left by the retreating tide. This was the stomach of the world, slit open and spread flat exposing a dull grey colour and veined texture: enzymes and juices left in the crevices and hollows of corrugated tissue.

Our life consisted of one trek after another over this boring landscape – why we did not stay in one spot was easily answerable: life then would become dull in the extreme – and it was during one of these wanderings that we encountered another nomad, one I hoped never to meet: the father of Stella's baby.

5

... for around those flecks of light float the lichen of space ...

Fridjt

Day had dawned through a cage of cirrus that covered the sky like an iron mask, and the sun's heat, controlled by the Soal thermostatic mushroom towers, allowed a rise of 5 degrees centigrade which went unnoticed by humans but caused all the Soal to waken virtually simultaneously: a most effective alarm. The nervous systems of the Soal were extremely sensitive to changes in temperature, which was why they had built the mushroom towers. They were not vulnerable to extremes in temperature provided they had time to adjust to them but any sudden changes, up or down the scale, would have a fatal effect upon their systems. Consequently the temperatures in the zones were tightly controlled and the Soal acclimatized in chambers on moving regions. The poles were left unvisited and remained frozen.

Stella and I were already out on the mud, breathing in the lovely morning stink of decaying vegetation and animal life. Gaseous bubbles of mud burst between our toes and the smell of stale sweat from our armpits created alternatives to the other odours.

I was asking (my unquenchable curiosity) about her personal affairs – her life before I had entered it, about which she was not over-talkative.

'Don't you ever wonder about your father?' I asked. 'I mean,' I hesitated, 'you don't even know what he looks like. From what you've told me of your promiscuous life, before we met, he could even be the father of your child ...' I stopped because she was staring at me so furiously she frightened me. I am not a big man but physical violence does not normally overawe me unless it is accompanied by passion and fury. Stella looked about to fly at me tooth and nail. However, she merely shifted the baby's position from one hip to the other. I watched the process, licking my lips nervously.

'My father,' she said finally, and very slowly, 'was one of the five men who terrorized the mudwalkers for six months. The Soal eventually caught them together. They were boiled alive and then thrown to the crabs.'

I found this difficult to believe, and felt she was over-dramatizing the execution of the men. So I said, 'That sounds extremely primitive for the Soal.'

Matter-of-factly she answered, 'Perhaps they thought they needed to put out a strong warning?'

I gave her a sideways look – in some ways Stella turned more soil with one thrust of a spade than I did after a long ploughing contemplation. Perhaps all women were naturally as astute. I had no way of knowing.

'But five men? They could not be afraid of a gathering of five unarmed mudwalkers.'

She gave me one of those superior smiles I had come to associate with female smugness and I realized that it was true – for a gathering of just Stella, myself and the baby girl would cause great alarm on the vat walks. Five men would amount to insurrection of no small nature. A thought occurred to me which I voiced out aloud.

'The Soal must have very weak defences.'

Stella smiled again.

'You should know about that. You've lived there.'

I said nothing for I was ashamed of the fact that the Soal defences, if they had any, were an unknown quantity to me. I had never had occasion to ask about them, and I doubted I would be informed if I had done. My violent thoughts had all been directed towards Endrod. It is difficult to entertain thoughts of revolution with only one head. These things need discussion. Revolution is forged out of many minds – at the most a single mind merely produces that substance from which the forging begins.

'Stella . . .' I was about to admit my failure when she held up a warning hand. I realized what was wrong and said rather superfluously :

'Quickly, put distance between us. Someone's coming. I told you we should not have walked together.'

However, before I could move a few paces Stella called out, 'It's all right. It's a human. I would know if it was the Soal.'

She pointed and I followed the finger. A long way off a man was plodding on mudshoes towards us. We waited, expecting him to veer off when he saw us but he continued using us as his target, and the nearer he approached, the more anxious I became – not because of the Soal Law, but because of Stella's reaction. She was watching him through narrowed eyes that bore obvious knowledge of the person they viewed.

'Who is it?' I asked quickly. I had a large blockage in my throat and my stomach was turning circles.

'A friend,' she said simply and then glanced possessively at the baby, which confirmed my suspicions.

'Will I,' I said, as casually as I could manage, 'will I have to fight him?'

Stella looked round, the eyes now widened. 'What for? Besides he would kill you.'

The man was quite close now and I saw what she meant. He was like a walking hill, huge and round, but not with fat – the muscles stood out in chunks on the broad expanse of his abdomen as he walked. Unlike my own, which hung free, his testicles were tied up between his legs. I guessed they were probably his only vulnerable piece of anatomy. Slung about his shoulders were two intricate fish traps.

When he was about ten metres from me I unslung the crossbow and wound the mechanism. The balding giant stopped short.

'That far and no farther,' I warned.

Stella slapped me hard across the arm with her free hand.

'Don't be stupid,' she shouted.

But I was resolute.

'I'll kill him before he makes another step,' I barked. 'Before he gets within arm's reach.'

The hill in front of me cracked across the face, the bent nose bending even further as the grin spread.

'She's my woman now,' I said.

The grin vanished. 'Oh, yes?'

Stella interrupted. 'He hasn't touched me Fridjt.'

The grin returned. 'Ah!' Fridjt took a step forward and I lifted the weapon level with his chest.

'Cave!' Stella's sharp voice made my finger tighten rather than relax.

'If you do, I shall walk away from you and never see you again.'

I hesitated. 'What about him then? He's the father of your child.'

'That's all he is.'

I shouted. 'You hear that, kraken?' I kicked off my mudshoes.

Finally the big man finished a sentence. 'You speak strange words for a mudwalker. I don't know what a kraken is but I do know that bolt won't stop me from cracking your neck – even if I have to crawl to you with it sticking outa m'chest.'

'Then I'll just have to split your nose in two,' I replied coolly, raising the bow to head height – Fridjt's head height that is.

Suddenly he threw his arms in the air.

'What've I done? Tell me? I might even say I'm sorry or something – if I only knew what I've done.'

Then he casually stepped forward, wrenched the crossbow from my grasp and with a huge hand in my face sent me sprawling backwards into the mud. I half spun round, skidding on the black mire. Fury unleashed in my brain: I had not had the courage to kill him when it came to the test. I climbed to my knees and went slipping and sliding across the mud, clawing at his legs. A fist struck me on the shoulder and again I went reeling, the wind breaking from my body. I heard him laughing. Stella was silent, almost sullen, watching us.

I climbed unsteadily to my feet again, my hands full of mud.

'You fornicator of empty whelkshells,' I said softly. Whether he understood or not he stepped forward, legs open to deliver a kick. I sent the mud splattering across his eyes with a quick flick of my right hand, at the same time bringing my foot up for a sharp kick at his vulnerables. My toes struck a hard protector – a clamshell or something similar, wrapped in the cloth. Nevertheless he winced, a thick leg reciprocated my action, and for me the world exploded.

I awoke later inside the segment of a needle. My head was full of the aftertaste of bad dreams and I had half an egg above one of my eyes.

'Eat something.' It was Stella about forty kilometres away, offering me boiled seaweed.

'Please,' I said waving her image away. 'No.'

'He kicked you in the head.'

'That means I have to eat seaweed?' I said. 'I don't even like the stuff when I'm well.'

'Eat it anyway.' A piece was dangled before my mouth and I feigned vomiting until it disappeared.

Slowly vision returned in the dim light. It must have been coming on night or we should not be together. I could see half the sun, a blurred fuzzy and misshapen cloud of red light. Fridjt came into focus in front of it.

'That hurt,' I said, pointing to the wound.

He was eating, and spluttered through a mouthful of cockles: 'So what are you going to do about it?'

I answered loftily. 'I don't see why I should reveal my plans to the enemy – that would seem to me to be an idiotic piece of military strategy. However, I should like you to consider whether you sleep light, or heavy, for in the answer to that question lies your future ...'

'Stop this,' Stella glared at us. 'Get a Continental and an Islander together and immediately there is antipathy. The Soal are our enemies – and no other.'

I stared at this remarkable woman.

'Where did you learn words like antipathy? I thought you had lived on the mudflats all your life.'

She was doing something with the baby – one of the innumerable cleansing or feeding tasks involved with raising an infant, and she looked up.

'I haven't always teamed up with dull minds like his,' she indicated Fridjt with a quick flick of a finger, 'or lack of moral courage like yours. Once ... there was a man whose intellect

31

dwarfed yours – which is not so very much – and whose body was purpose built for physical exactitude. We loved together for two years – unfortunately there was no child. I think I was too young.'

'And I think I'm disgusted,' I said, turning to the wall. 'Of course your hero was giant size if you knew him when you were that young. They all are at that age. I expect he never did any wrong – how did you lose him?'

'There's no need to be jealous, Cave,' she said softly. 'He too was from the Soal like yourself – a Continental. He died of an illness.'

Fridjt was regarding this conversation without interest, viewing each party as we spoke, and chewing solemnly upon his food. Finally, without changing his expression, he asked, 'Who's dull?'

I giggled and Stella smiled. Then I said, 'We had better go to different segments to sleep,' and left them together. I was too befogged by Fridjt's blow to worry. Anyway, it certainly would not be the first time for them.

I fell asleep almost at once, but later, feeling drugged with a heavy sleep, I was awoken by someone pressing against me.

'Wha ... what is it?' I mumbled.

'It's me ... Stella. It's time we ... we consummated our to-getherness.'

I came awake. Her breasts were squashed hard against my ribs and a hand was doing something between my legs.

'What about ...?'

'Nothing. He is nothing.' Her breath was hot and musty-smelling near my nostrils.

'You are my man now. Take me. Weyym wants you to take me. I'm a lusty woman and I need it now.'

'I don't know how,' I whined.

The answer was in physical form, delivered furiously, but whether in violent anger or passion I could not ascertain, my own feelings being somewhat confused. I submitted.

Later, when we had finished, there was an electrical storm – one of the kind where the lightning burns across the sky in thousands of thin bows of light. It was a bad one and the webs of light blotted out the stars with their brightness when they flashed.

'It's as if there were a cage of fire around the world,' I said, marvelling at the changing networks, the patterns that the lightning formed. Stella moaned something.

'What?' I asked, thinking she was afraid of the storm.

'Bastards,' she said, loudly now. Then she turned her head towards me and buried her face in my chest. Poor Stella – she blamed the Soal for everything, even natural phenomena.

The meteorites that sometimes accompanied storms such as this flared like momentary stars as they hit the atmosphere at the point where the storm was raging. This was only the second straight-lightning storm I had seen in my life, and I was enjoying it tremendously. Stella was no lover of beauty, otherwise she would have conquered her fear and joined me in viewing the splendid spectacle.

6

... lichen is the first upon the rock – it is the foundation ...

Death

That night the baby died. It was not neglect on Stella's part – not because we spent the middle hours together. The nameless mite had been getting thinner for several days, having diarrhoea and probably a number of other unseen complaints. Stella did not seem surprised or bitter at the news – she told me it was the second baby she had lost. The first had been in the foetus stage. Infant mortality was high amongst us humans. Before a shambling and broken-voiced Fridjt brought us the news (he had been looking after the child while Stella and I had lain together, and seemed to take the small death harder than anyone) we had been lying in the dark, after the storm had abated, talking to each other.

'Did you like that?' Stella questioned me concerning our consummation.

'It was better than walking the vats after the sludge has been freshly turned,' I replied in a satisfied tone and squeezing her thigh.

She rolled away from me, angry.

'If that's what you think of my mating you can wait until the season comes around and take your chances with the other females,' she snapped huffily.

'No! No!' I was bewildered. 'Don't take that attitude, please. I really do like walking the vats – or did.'

'Really?' Her hand touched my shoulder in the darkness. 'What else was it like?'

'It was like soaring to the sky,' I replied. 'It was as if my life, having been hammered flat by misfortune, had been reshaped into something mysteriously meaningful – a multi-faceted shape constructed from light and dark, and pulsing with power. It was ...'

'You don't need to convince me further,' she replied, 'but tell me, why do you like the vat walks? I've heard of them but never seen them. Do they really cover a quarter of Brytan?'

I thought for a bit then replied, 'I suppose they must do. An awful waste I suppose when you consider ...'

'Consider what?'

'Well, the number of Soal that use them.'

We talked like this for many hours until the light of day was thrown through the translucent walls by that fuzzy ball that rolls around its sky. It sparkled on the crystal needle towers we could see from the segment, colours dancing in the mud. The tidal change was due in two or three hours so there was no point in moving. Fridjt would probably lay his traps and catch us a few fish for breakfast. At least I hoped he would. Fridjt was very proud of his traps – they were intricately made and finely balanced mechanisms, constructed of rustless metal. They never failed to attract the fish into their mirrored passages. When expanded and set they covered a full cubic metre of ocean, finding the depth of the shoals automatically, but they folded down to a mere twenty centimetres in length and two in radius, for carrying purposes, and were light and easy to handle. A true work of Soal craftsmanship.

This generous aspect of the Soal was somewhat difficult to understand now that I was a mudwalker. While I had been the companion and servant of Lintar I never questioned such enigmatic behaviour. It seemed natural then that our benevolent masters should find pleasure in occasionally distributing aid to the pathetic humans on the mud, but now I was on the receiving end such acts seemed strangely at variance with the Soal policy of killing humans whenever a legitimate reason showed itself.

For instance we had the needle towers, provisioned with a unit that converted seawater into fresh water, at the same time introducing human vitamin needs into the supply. This at least ensured that our basic requirements, beyond food, were met. In the slim crystal towers we had comparative warmth during the chilling night exhalations, safety from drowning and solar units for heating food.

If the Soal wanted to destroy us all, they need only have removed the towers.

My deductions produced a line of thought.

The towers and handouts were established at a time when the Soal had no need to be cautious. The policy of genocide was the result of a change in these circumstances.

The towers were self-maintaining and required nothing more than supervision by the Soal, to ensure that humans were not gathering in groups of two or more.

Destruction of the towers was an action to be avoided for the present, one to be saved until absolutely necessary. Until that time, open slaughter was a crudeness unworthy of a master race.

The whittling down of the human population by apparent legitimate policing was an interim measure and should the situation worsen (whatever that situation was), more drastic moves would have to be taken.

I voiced my opinions to Stella, whose own opinion of me was very low as a result.

'Why didn't you find out the answers to these questions yourself, when you were with the Soal?' she demanded.

'Because they didn't concern me then – and don't forget the Soal do not speak Terran to each other. I had no idea what passed between them in the council chambers. I can't hear through locked doors, even though I can mouth read. They *were* worried about something, *perpetually* – consequently it was a normal state of affairs and not one that struck me as in need of investigation. Finally, I was hardly ever allowed out of the Klees's house – certainly not without an escort.'

So I defended myself, but it did not save me from her scorn.

While her tirade was in progress Fridjt entered carrying the child. He no longer looked an ogre – more like a crestfallen child himself. Stella turned a face of stone onto the small body, lying like a limp fish in the large man's hands.

'She's dead,' said Fridjt simply, but it sounded more like a question than a statement. He placed the infant carefully on one of the bunks and we all moved towards the door. The tower would dispose of the body, as it did with waste food and dead animals. Anything that generated the kind of bacteria that infested dead flesh was a usable commodity. The Soal could use it but I did not tell Stella that. She would have eaten the child rather than let it benefit the Soal.

We gathered our few belongings together and prepared to leave the tower, each of us lost in our own thoughts. Perhaps it was because we were all so preoccupied that we did not hear the approaching military. Stella went out first.

7

... upon which other lifeforms build ...

Murder

Stella returned quickly to warn us of approaching Soal but we were somewhat disorientated – after the death of the baby and by the time we had gathered our thoughts towards separation it was too late.

The vehicle hovered just outside the entrance to our segment and we knew we had been seen. There was nothing we could do – we stood, still as the infant behind us, waiting for the inevitable. A few moments later the entrance admitted a Soal – one of the hard-faced military. A painted gold bar running from his hands to his claw-like feet, along the edge of his skinwings, proclaimed him to be an officer. We were finished.

'Look,' I started desperately, 'this is not what you think, Poston-Yarcave.' I used his full rank to show him he was not dealing with an ignorant mudwalker – my own name was a shortened version of that rank. 'We were all in separate segments when we heard your craft. We ... we panicked.' I laughed. 'You can understand that.'

The Soal officer ran his eyes over our group, then said in Terran, 'You are the human, Cave?'

I laughed again, slapping my knee.

'Yes, yes. You know me then? You've seen me with Lintar?' I tried for a recognition but could not place him. His feathers rose irritably.

'I am from the continent. We have a call for your arrest – from Librarian Endrod.'

I was stunned, and turned to look at the other two. Fridjt was standing quietly, his arms folded. Stella stared straight ahead. I could read nothing from either of their expressions. I turned back to the officer.

'But I haven't broken any laws,' I raised my hands in the Soal gesture for honesty. 'Not since I was banished.'

The officer smiled in that detestable way the Soal have, by twisting the upper beak over the lower. His small eyes took in the three of us together. His meaning was plain.

'But,' I cried, 'you didn't know that I'd be with someone. You couldn't know that.'

Stella said dully, 'They don't need an excuse these days Cave. If they want to arrest you, they simply do that. There's little justice on the mud.'

I whirled round again angrily.

'I have friends,' I waved my crossbow in the air.

Suddenly the second Soal was behind the first, in the entrance to the segment. He was saying something in his own language. I read it, automatically, over the officer's shoulder.

'What is the trouble? You are a long time here.'

The officer did not answer – instead he turned to us and said, 'Get on the mud – all of you.'

I realized then that we were finished and made a move towards the door, half-turning to pass a look at the others to say in a gesture, 'I did my best.' Stella's face had a peculiar look on it which pulled me up short.

'Stella?' I said in a low voice.

Her eyes glittered with a kind of triumph.

'They're together,' she muttered in a satisfied tone. 'Your bow.'

I wound the mechanism without really considering why. The Soal officer looked puzzled but stood his ground. He had no reason to move.

'On the mud,' he jerked out the words again, annoyed at having to repeat himself. No one moved except Fridjt who took a step forward.

'Kill them!' rapped Stella.

I gasped, unbelieving. No mudwalker had ever used violence against a Soal – not for as long as I could remember. The Soal memories contained the same thoughts as my own, for they merely began ruffling their feathers in anger. They did not even bear personal arms – though the craft contained brainstingers.

'Now!' screamed Stella, stamping her foot. 'Do it, you fools, do it now.'

Fridjt suddenly came to life again, reached forward and grabbed the officer by his right skinwing, tearing the flimsy webbing. The Soal opened his mouth in pain and Fridjt clamped his hand round the mouth, between the two beaklike jaws, and drove the head against the wall, shattering the light skull.

I stood transfixed in terror, shaking from head to foot. The other Soal took off from the ledge and began gliding towards his craft, which was hovering a few metres from the tower.

'Get him,' shouted Stella.

I raised the crossbow, levelled the sights on the moving figure and pulled the trigger. There was a smooth clunk and a nudge from the crossbow as the bolt left the channel. I was trembling so much I felt I must have missed, but the figure doubled-up in mid-air and fell to the mud below with a muffled splatter. He gave one twist, as he lay in the small hole his impact had made, and was then still. We could see the black bolt projecting from beneath his torn armpit. The amount in view, and the angle of the bolt, told me that the point of it was buried somewhere in the Soal's brain. I shivered involuntarily.

'We're really in trouble now,' I stammered still staring at the body below.

The way the Soal had fallen into the mud reminded me of poor Askreenata, when her wings had failed her over the sludge of the vats. She plummeted in the same manner – broken-winged and with a look of surprise mixed with annoyance, that changed to terror when she hit the surface of the mire. Unlike the Soal below, her death was one of suffocation, watched by helpless playmates. A Soal feared death only when it was imminent. Until that last second, they were immortal.

Stella snorted. 'We were dead anyway.'

'Yes but . . .' I could not find the words. There was no punishment great enough for such a dastardly crime as ours, but I was sure the Soal would think of one.

Fridjt spoke for the first time since the nightmare began. 'Come. We must go quickly.' He was no longer the bumbling idiot. It was I who lacked the mental strength necessary to meet the situation.

'Where?' I cried. 'They'll find us wherever we go on the mud – there's nowhere to hide.' I began babbling but neither of them were listening to me. They were staring at the hovering machine, divorced from us by just a few metres of unbridgeable air.

'We've got to get on that chiton craft,' said Stella. Then she jerked her thumb at me.

'He can control it.'

A heavy feeling settled in my stomach as I stared helplessly, and silently now, at these humans that had destroyed me within a matter of days. They were alien beings – I did not understand either of them and I doubted I ever would, but I was grateful to them now, as surely as if we three were grafted together. Between them they had seen to it that any hope I ever cherished of returning to my comfortable life on the mainland was gone now. Even Lintar would be horrified at what his once close human companion had done.

'How are we to reach it?' I asked them helplessly.

'You think of a way,' said Fridjt, nodding his huge balding head at me. 'You're the one with the brains. I'll give you thirty seconds – then I'm going to throw you at the chiton and if you don't make it, well then, you fall.'

Chiton was the mudwalker's name for a Soal patrol vehicle – they called it that because it was built with overlapping plates of metal and was roughly the same shape as that creature.

'... fifteen, sixteen ...'

'All right! All right! I'll think of something,' I snapped. 'Just be quiet for a moment and let me concentrate.'

It took me more than the allowed time to find the answer but when I did it was a good one.

8

... My eyes see no right or wrong ...

Soal

Endrod walked along the cold stone corridors with the characteristic featherlight step of a Soal. Had he been human his brow would have been furrowed and a smouldering anger evident in his complexion. Being a Soal he expressed his inner rage by blowing hard through the vents behind his tiny mushroom ears and ruffling his coat. Endrod had just been refused a third request for licence to commit immediate genocide upon the remainder of what was once an intelligent, resourceful race. The Klees of Brytan and Hess had vetoed the act.

Endrod came to the balcony and, contrary to normal safety observations, spread his bat-like wings and glided over the courtyard. Soal did not normally take risks by gliding over a hard surface from two storeys up, for the adult Soal had long since given up soaring for fun. It was indicative of the ill-humour of Endrod. He hit the grass on the far side of the courtyard rather harder than he intended and toppled awkwardly on to his back. He was finding his feet just as another Soal entered the courtyard.

'Opanion,' Endrod spoke before the other could express the obvious surprise she felt at seeing her superior rolling around on the grass. 'What do you do here?'

Opanion was unruffled by the terse attitude of the Librarian. She was used to his bouts of bad temper.

'I came to tell you that your wish has been granted, Chief Librarian Endrod,' said the other. She was the Assistant Chief Librarian, and it was her wish that Endrod regain his former position as Head of the Military in order that she herself might be promoted to her Chief's present position. She was ambitious, but only in her own field. Chief Librarian would suit her fine.

'Oh? What wish is that?' the Chief Librarian asked, his anger less evident.

'The mudwalkers have done something which may help you regain your former rank. They have killed two Soal – one of the killers is believed to be your old antagonist's son – the human Cave.'

Endrod was eager to hear the whole story and Opanion repeated what she had heard in the communications cell. The Hessian Soal had found the bodies of a Yarcave and Teel at one of the needle towers near the coast. Shortly before that a Soal craft was seen entering a transcontinental tube, heading towards one of the southern oceans. It was guessed that the human called Cave was piloting the craft, since he was the only human in the north that had lived amongst the Soal and would have the expertise.

'Cave,' breathed Endrod deeply. 'I have him at last.'

Opanion offered nothing, for the Chief Librarian suddenly went into the Soal position of deep concentration with the head pulled deep down between the equivalent of the human clavicles. Opanion waited patiently for Endrod to come out. Finally the Chief Librarian surfaced again.

He said, 'Who is conducting the search for the fugitives?'

'Kaltan, head of the Ostraylean military,' answered Opanion.

'That's good,' continued Endrod. 'He is a particular friend of mine being from the same string of eggs.' The Soal females laid a string of capsule-shaped eggs once every three tours. These were left in a public room to be visited by various males who pierced one of the leather-shelled eggs at random, fertilizing it. Thus several Soal might have the same mother but different fathers. The male cared for the egg during the period prior to hatching and the mother played no more part in the welfare of her offspring. It was only during reproduction that the Soal discriminated between their sexes. At all other times the gender was disregarded. Endrod was a male and Opanion a female but apart from their hidden sexual organs, there was no physical difference between them. No Soal would take gender into account when considering anything but the laying and fertilizing of eggs. Comradeship was not unknown amongst them, but romantic love was. The Soal considered the human males and females as two entirely different species – they felt more comfortable with that idea, though they knew it to be untrue.

Endrod said, 'I want you to go to him and ask him to delay the search for the natives until I arrive there. The Klees of Ostraylea is still here, for the annual conference is not yet over. I will ask leave of absence to join him in his homeward journey tomorrow. It is a long time since I visited the southern hemisphere so there will be nothing suspicious in my request. Now you go.'

Opanion left to make preparations for his trip. Endrod made his way to his own chambers.

Once in his rooms he took a favourite crossbow from the wall upon which it hung to serve as an ornamentation and then called for a junior librarian to accompany him upon a long hunting trip.

The annual Conference of the Klees was nearing its close and the twenty-four Klees had once again given a majority vote in favour of allowing those humans that were alive to remain so – apart from any law-breakers amongst them. It was a small insurance against an accident of the future. The majority vote was becoming smaller each year, however, and the Klees of Brytan, the leader of the moderates, feared that the extremists would soon gain fuller support. It was argued by the latter group that humans were wasteful, in that they devoured flesh by the pound, whereas a Soal would make a decaying piece of meat last until the maggots finally consumed it. Humans also required constant surveillance to prevent revolt and this was an exhausting task for the Soal military, whose numbers were decreasing rather than growing. The Soal race, as a whole, was shrinking because of sexual indolence. Reproduction was a duty, not a pleasure, and duties were becoming distasteful things that wasted valuable relaxation time.

Soal public opinion held that the Earth was a safe little nest, and nothing could possibly harm them, except perhaps the internal problems created by humans. Destroy the humans, and all would be placid and unruffled security. Why bother keeping numbers at their maximum if it was unnecessary? Of course there would need to be a minimum population for the species to perpetuate – but the actual figure could be decided upon when the numbers fell nearer to danger level. It was only by skilful oratory that the Klees of Brytan had managed to persuade the majority of the other Klees that the slaughter of humans was not a course to embark upon at that time.

The world was segregated into twenty-four sections between latitudes 60° North and 60° South. Each segment was of the same size, and whether it consisted of water or of land was of no consideration. The Klees of Brytan was no less important than the Klees of Central Aysea, even though the latter's territory consisted entirely of continental land mass and the Klees of Brytan had included in his area many thousands of useless acres of ocean. In fact, policing was more difficult work for the Klees of Brytan as humans were permitted to live only on small islands and wasteland.

The land outside the 60° latitudes, the poles, part of Kanadar, Skandanayvea and Usser, was not under the direct control of the Klees, but those who had territories that bordered these places helped to police them for any humans that might be forming bands. Like the Soal, humans had an inherent magnetism that drew them together.

The main item on the agenda for the conference was the fracture of one of the spars on the Ostraylean mushroom tower. The Klees of Ostraylea required consent to gather humans to repair the damage. Asked why the humans were needed he said that though much of the work could be carried out by machines, certain tasks required the dexterity, strength and intelligence of a human. In the network of towers which maintained a fairly constant temperature over the surface of the Earth, a single tower was highly important; Soal could live for only a short time in varying temperatures. As part of a network, each tower was in itself a keystone, but they also did another job – a far more important one which was revealed only to Soal of a certain rank. Like humans the Soal placed little trust in each other as individuals. Endrod had proved untrustworthy in once giving the secret to a human in the hope that the human would have to die. Instead the knowledge was wiped clean from both their minds and Endrod was left with an intense hatred for the humans who he knew had been responsible for his demotion.

9

... I see only life climbing on life ...

Tangiia

There was a sail, a long way off on the horizon, cutting across the blue water like the dorsal fin of a giant fish. We watched it, running with the wind, and envied its helmsman the freedom and joy of reckless speed.

This was a different ocean from the one we had known – the water was of a blue glass and seemed as if it would shatter when a stone was tossed onto its surface. There was a tide but no mud – just a bed of jagged rocks and sand.

When the water was full, up to the lip of the island, we could bathe in it and watch the fish – fish of many shapes and colours – darting about amongst a hard, multi-hued rock which grew like a plant beneath the water.

Stella was enthralled with our new environment and I could see that Fridjt did not dislike it either. We still had to dodge the Soal whenever they came near to the island, but it was so easy to hide amongst the foliage which covered the land. In any case, the Soal did not seem to be interested in thorough searches for they never went overhead at all; they just skirted the beaches. There was evidence of human occupation on the island, but the owner of the house and other human artifacts was not present. We suspected that since the possessions appeared to have been recently in use that the owner was away – probably it was the mating period in this part of the world.

There was one particular type of tree, the most prevalent variety, which fascinated me. It grew large nuts which contained a liquid that was delicious to drink; Stella called the tree a palm. (Stella, I had since learned, was quite knowledgeable about the Old World before the Soal. The women, it seemed, passed on stories of the Old World to their daughters and in this way retained a small amount of our history. There would have been no point in telling the stories to a son – men had no one to whom they could retell the tale, since it was the mothers that kept the children.)

Fridjt continually remarked that the air was clean and fresh on the island, something that did nothing to enhance the place as far as I, a breather of what Stella called 'the foul atmospheres of the Soal muck pits', was concerned. Once, she caught me deeply inhaling the delightful fumes from a rotting fish that I had found on the beach, and she became quite angry, abusing my mother and calling me a 'Soal shitsmeller.' She terminated her vicious verbal attack with a slap. After that episode I tried to cure myself of the habit.

After a time it became obvious to the three of us that the sailing craft, a very sleek vehicle that seemed to ride the air some two or three centimetres above the water, was heading towards the island. Man is at his most beautiful cutting through the air in one of his own creations. This man was sitting at the rear of his craft managing the steering mechanism. As the craft drew closer we hid in the foliage, for the occupant would attempt to kill us if we confronted him directly, on his own territory.

'I shall hold him,' said Fridjt, 'while you try to talk him into our way of thinking. If it seems useless, we shall have to kill him.'

'Or her,' I corrected.

'Him,' said Stella, emphatically, nodding towards the boat.

The man, and it was a man, was standing up in the craft now and we could see that our earlier viewing of the boat's capabilities had resulted in illusions : it did not ride above the waves but instead skimmed their crests. It gave me a peculiar sensation in my stomach to watch the voyager hopping from wave-top to wave-top and my single experience of a ride on the ocean's surface as a boy left me in no doubt as to how I should feel as a passenger in the craft.

As the boat skipped over the submerged white wall, from the waves to the calmer water close to the island, the newcomer swiftly dropped the sail and glided in, with the momentum, to slide onto the sand. Jumping out he secured the craft by pulling it up the beach. Then he turned and began to walk towards us. We noticed he was limping and one eye had a huge dark swelling beneath it; mating wounds, I had no doubt.

We waited by the path that led to his primitive dwelling, the tension high between us. We heard him pushing the fronds of the larger plants aside as he walked and he was grumbling about something to himself. Suddenly he stopped and looked about him curiously. My heart began to race. He suspected something and he was a big man, almost as large as Fridjt; also a weapon hung from a thong at his waist: a piece of hard wood studded with sharp teeth along each edge. He would be a difficult man to take on in an open frontal attack.

However, after a grunt he continued down the overgrown path, slightly more cautiously than before. I hugged the shadowy, dark floor of the jungle and waited until I heard him pass – then a gargle fell on my ears and looking up I saw Fridjt had him by the throat from behind and was trying to pull him down.

The islander was immensely strong and Fridjt hung on to the man's neck with his full weight off the ground for a few seconds, while the pair of them swayed on the jungle track. Then, as the islander tried to prise open Fridjt's fingers, he fell to the floor with the mudwalker on top. There was a brief struggle, but mating had left the man weak and by the way his eyes suddenly widened I could tell that Fridjt had gripped him by the testicles and was applying pressure.

'No!' he shouted.

'Not crush – kill me first.' His dialect was strange but we understood the words.

Stella answered. 'No one will hurt you if you do as I tell you.'

I glanced at Stella quickly. How easily she assumed the role of leader, without really having anything else, no physical strength or powerful mind, to offer.

'Get his weapon Cave,' grunted Fridjt, the exertion evident in his voice. They were obviously a match for each other. I quickly bent down and yanked the strange dagger from the islander's waist, snapping the thong.

'Get that cord around his hands,' snapped Stella. I did as I was told, though he struggled violently under Fridjt's adhesive grip. Once we had him tied we sat him against one of the trees and Stella spoke to him in a soothing voice.

'We won't hurt you, as long as you don't try to attack us,' she said gently.

'We will die,' he sniffed back at her, his broad face sullen. 'We will all die when Soal catch us together.'

I said, 'They won't. We'll hide in the plants.'

He found this rather funny and laughed.

'Jungle will not hide us. They can see through Jungle with their machine.'

We all looked at one another and I wiped a brow suddenly wet with perspiration. We had trusted that the leaves would conceal us: viewers had not been used on the mud. We had been an ace away from discovery. The Soal obviously thought that all humans in this area would be mating at that time and only made cursory inspections of the beaches.

'We mustn't make another mistake like that,' said Stella thoughtfully. 'But if you do get caught together, any of you, then I suggest you start fighting each other immediately. The fight would have to terminate with one of you dying, of course, otherwise the Soal will know you are not serious. Therefore I suggest the fight is in earnest. That way one of you will live.'

I nodded, being the weakest man, to show that I accepted this as the only sensible action in such circumstances, though I was virtually agreeing to throw my life away.

I swallowed and finished off her little speech.

'The Soal will be told by the survivor that the other man was trespassing. But what about you? Shall we start becoming amorous or what?'

Stella answered swiftly. 'That would not work. I take my chances the same as you two – and I warn you now, I fight dirty.'

We protested but she insisted that it was the only way to handle an emergency.

'However, these are extreme measures – for use only in the last ditch. For now we must find a place to hide out, where the Soal can't see us.'

There was a noise on the ground behind us. We had forgotten our captive and he was now on his feet. We watched him warily, Fridjt especially, and waited to see if he would make a run for it. Instead he spoke.

'I will show you place,' he promised.

His eyes were wide apart on his broad clean-shaven face – deep brown eyes above flaring nostrils. It was, even taking into account my limited experience of my fellow humans, a most dishonest face.

'Don't let him loose,' I warned. 'He'll butcher the lot of us.'

But the other two had no intention of setting him free, though I could tell that Stella was quite taken with him. When I questioned her about it she said that he was big and strong and would come in useful to us once we had convinced him that humans should begin banding together against the Soal. I had not, until that moment, realized that we were 'banding together' against anyone, but once I thought about it I agreed with her. The new man's knowledge of the local geography would be invaluable to us.

However, we kept him tied and made him walk ahead of us. He led the way through what he called 'my trees' to a small escarpment some three hundred metres high. On the top of the westward spur was a crack approximately a metre in width and ten metres long. Subsequently this proved to be the entrance to an old volcanic fault which, after a gradual descent, angled sharply some thirty metres downwards. The wall of the hole had wooden stakes driven into it which were ranged in the form of a ladder to enable users to climb to the very bottom, where the shaft opened up into a cavern. Here, Tangiia, as we learned his name to be, told us we would be safe from Soal eyes. He had learned through experience that viewers could only penetrate to a certain depth. Flint-lit torches made the air somewhat unbreathable but in future it would be better for us to sit in the dark and talk, and climb out by using our sense of touch, feeling our way from rung to rung. We learned that Tangiia had hidden his mother there when she returned to visit him thirty or forty months after he had reached independence. He did not say what had happened to her.

'Well done,' said Stella to Tangiia, looking around the cavern with satisfaction. Her slim nude body with its bell-shaped breasts was throwing a very inviting shadow upon the white wall of the hideout. I ran my tongue over my front teeth. It was quite an intimate little home we had been offered by our new man. Stella saw my eyes ranging over her glistening flesh and then glancing down at the hay-strewn floor.

'We'll rest for a while,' she ordered. 'Put out the torches. We needn't worry about him,' she pointed at Tangiia. 'He can't climb out with his hands tied behind his back.'

The torches were extinguished and I lay on the floor where I had stood, and waited. After a while I began to get a little anxious – she had not moved. Or perhaps, the ugly thought snapped out, she was lying with one of the other men? Just when I felt my anger was going to scream from my mouth, uncontrollably, in a torrent of abuse, I felt wet warm buttocks pressing against my abdomen.

'Now!' she hissed close to my ear as she arched her neck backwards.

'This way round?' I whispered, surprised.

'This is the way animals do it,' she replied, 'and I feel like an animal.'

I think she was disappointed, at first, in my gentle performance, but I felt inhibited because I knew the others could hear our movements. However, I too was eager towards the end, and ceased to care whether the other men were there or not.

Some minutes later I heard Tangiia whispering in sepulchral tones to himself, 'I found you my Peloa. I found you again – and again I left you on belly of sea.'

'Keep quiet,' grunted Fridjt impiously, 'we're all trying to sleep.'

10

... first the lichen, then moss, grasses, flowers, insects, birds ...

Endrod

The dauntlessness of man is not quenched by five thousand months of alien rule: Tangiia was not in the cavern when we awoke. At first we thought he might be hiding in some dark corner but, joining hands and walking the whole floor space, which was only about twenty metres square, we realized he was missing.

We climbed the rude ladder, Fridjt first, fully expecting the exit to be blocked and a triumphant Tangiia to be jeering at us from the outside. As we neared the exit, no light greeted us and Fridjt said, 'He's done it. We're locked in.' Panic surged through my chest, but just as it was about to gain control of my limbs Fridjt shouted, 'It's all right. It's night and the hole's clear.'

We stumbled gratefully out onto the ridge. It occurred to me only later that Tangiia could have been waiting with a weapon, and have pounced then. It would only have been necessary to finish Fridjt. Stella and I were no match for him and could have been left for later.

The three of us made our way through the trees and finally came upon Tangiia. He was sitting with his back towards us, in front of a fire, and his hands were free. A closer inspection showed them to be bloody and scratched – no doubt the result of scraping the thongs against a piece of rough rock.

While Fridjt and I hesitated, hovering in the shadows, Stella stepped out boldly and sat beside the sullen figure with rounded brown shoulders. He said nothing to her, just sat staring into the flames. Stella began speaking to him in a low voice, inaudible to Fridjt and me, and after a while we saw him look up but there was no change of expression on his face. Then he slowly shook his head and drew a finger across his eyes.

Stella stood up and came back to where we stood.

'It's no good,' she said. 'I can't get him to join us or sanction our staying here. He's worried about the consequences.'

'Then we'll have to kill him,' growled Fridjt roughly.

'I told him that,' Stella answered.

'He just shrugged his shoulders. I also promised that if we stayed we would find him a woman – one for him and one for Fridjt.'

This statement lifted a certain amount of my doubts about our remaining as a group. I almost began feeling light-headed.

'And he refused the offer?'

Stella replied, 'He didn't even answer.'

We stood staring at one another for a few minutes and I could see that a decision had formed itself in the minds of the other two. Then Fridjt nodded at Stella and with a grim expression on his round countenance he began walking towards Tangiia, taking care not to let his feet make any sound. Just then Stella raised a hand and seemed to concentrate on something. Then she hissed, 'Soal.'

Fridjt froze and looked at her face. Then the three of us began running back towards the crack on the hill. It took a little time to find the hole in the dark, but we did, and managed to scramble down into the security of our hay-floored nest again. The belly of a rock-lined world is a comforting place when you are hunted by a ruthless predator.

We were prepared to wait in the hole as long as necessary – but how long is *necessary*? Would Tangiia come and tell us when the Soal had gone (if indeed they had ever arrived – we only had Stella's intuition to guide us)? I doubted he would come.

Have you ever sat, in the darkness, and waited for something that you were sure was not going to happen? Time slows down, almost to a stop.

I waited, and waited, my hands tying knots with themselves and my mind counting my heartbeats. Finally I could not take any more.

'I'm going up,' I said, jumping to my feet.

'No,' cried Stella. 'Stop him Fridjt!'

But it was pitch black and Fridjt was clumsy. I was halfway up the ladder while he was still crashing about below thinking I was still there. At the entrance hole I paused, but having come so far I was not going to return without information.

My progress was slow but as I neared the clearing where we had left Tangiia I heard voices – one of which was in the halting, high-pitched accents of a Soal.

I went down on my chest and eased my way through the undergrowth, making sure not to make any noise – Soal hearing was not exceptional at low frequencies, but it was still able.

Once I could see some figures I paused. The fire had died considerably since the alarm had been given, and now just a red glow lit the figures that surrounded it. I counted – there were four Soal, all armed, and Tangiia. Probably there were another one or two Soal in the craft, which I could not see.

Suddenly I heard a voice which I recognized, and one which made my heart pound inside my chest. It was the second Soal to the left of Tangiia that had spoken. I stared hard at this alien but the light was too dim for me to be sure. Then Tangiia truculently kicked a log, making it flare and my eyes, not having moved, immediately recognized the features of my old enemy Endrod. The sight left me trembling and I cowered in the grass, burying my head deep into its roots.

I stayed in the same attitude for some time – until I felt a tap on my shoulder and looked up in relief to see Fridjt kneeling by my side. The Soal had gone and Stella was standing beside Tangiia, who had a broad grin stretching his already wide mouth. I climbed to my feet and when he saw me he came lumbering over and hugged me with his huge sweaty arms.

'My friend,' he cried joyfully. 'You killed Soal,' the last word was uttered in admiration.

I pointed accusingly at Fridjt.

'So did he,' I answered excitely.

'But you,' Tangiia laughed, now holding me at arm's length, 'you are brave one. He,' a hand flicked in Fridjt's direction, 'is big and strong and does not think too well. With him it is almost mistake.'

Funnily enough Fridjt did not take exception to this remark – in fact the fat fool grinned too. I had to suffer a vice-like but supposedly playful squeeze on my shoulder from that direction.

'How you kill this Soal?' asked Tangiia. 'Tell me friend, how you kill this stink-sucking birdman? You rip his wings off, yes?'

'Firstly,' I replied, backing away out of reach of his loving arms, 'I'm not your friend, though I realize it is probably the only affectionate term you know, and secondly I am not used to story telling – however in this instance I'll make an exception.'

'You tell me, but not so long words,' he smiled.

So I told him all the events that led up to the killing of the Soal officer and his companion and then proceeded to relate the way in which we escaped.

'. . . the vehicle was hovering just outside our segment – perhaps some five metres from the ledge. This was too far to jump but Stella had an idea. We tore the blanket given me by Lintar into strips and tied them together, forming a rope. Then Fridjt here took this up to the ledge of the segment above, and lowered it. I wrapped it around my waist and Fridjt began swinging me like a pendulum . . .'

'What is pendulum?'

I looked around me and saw a piece of vine a few metres away. Walking towards it I grasped it and used the end to demonstrate the principle – Tangiia understood and I continued.

'As Fridjt built up the swinging motion I was reaching out for the side of the craft, but on each return the makeshift rope bent on the top of the segment's entrance and crashed me against the ceiling. I have a thousand bruises to prove it. At last then, I went far enough out to get handholds on the craft but it was only after enormous effort – I am not a fit man – that I was able to pull myself up and into the craft. Once inside I had the job of controlling the vehicle – fortunately the controls are extremely simple and I'd seen them managed several times before, though I'd never actually piloted a craft myself. Freeing myself of the rope I then took the craft as close as I dared to the needle tower without mishap, allowing these two to jump inside. Then we set off, over the mud, admittedly a little erratically as I found the accelerator very finely tuned.

'It was difficult to decide what to do from that point onwards – all we had previously been concerned with was escaping from the immediate vicinity of the crime. We obviously wanted to go as far from the mud as possible but the Soal chiton was constructed only for local flight – not for long distance journeys. Then Stella remembered the Schooter tubes.'

I described the tubes to Tangiia, whose face immediately registered recognition of the structures that had patterned the world's surface for several thousand months.

The Schooter tubes were of human, not Soal, construction and though the Soal still used them occasionally the aliens were not great wanderers and the tubes were idle most of the time. They consisted of starting cannons, which were self-activating, and repeaters. A vehicle that entered a horizontally-pointing starter cannon from the rear merely had to wait until the breach was closed by a pressure door before being fired onto a repeater tube at something like three thousand kilometres an hour. The repeater, or booster tubes, each around a quarter of a kilometre long, were lined across continents and oceans to form snakes of silver with parted, segmented bodies. The presence of a vehicle in a cannon was recognized by the mechanism and the firing procedure automatically took place. Stella had known about the tubes from her former continental boy friend – at least she had known about the starting procedure and that the tubes could be angled manually by entering the wheelhouses situated on the top of each section, but neither of us had known how to control the duration of the journey.

We had cruised over the sea wall in our vehicle, hoping that those who saw us would believe the craft to be piloted by Soal. We had then entered the first Schooter tube starter cannon we came across and had begun a very distressing journey that made Fridjt and me violently ill.

When it came to stopping the problem solved itself – we came out over a large group of islands. I had decided to head south for I had an idea that we were over the Maldeas in the Endean Ocean. We had flown low, skimming over the water, when I recognized an island at the top of a peninsula and we had turned south-east into the Pasific Ocean, which I knew to be peppered with small islands.

Once we had found a suitable spot we landed and then covered the craft with branches and leaves. It was not a very thorough job but it was the best we could have done in the circumstances. Later, we decided, we could make better work of the camouflage.

All this I related to Tangiia, who stopped me several times, mainly because of my inability to simplify my explanations, or to clear up a word he did not understand. His vocabulary, like Fridjt's, was very limited, due to the lack of contact with other humans. The reason our language had managed to survive at all was because childhood learning was refreshed at mating periods and also the Soal military liked to talk as much as any human.

When I had finished, I asked Tangiia what the Soal had wanted, even though I was sure that Endrod was pursuing us, and had calculated our approximate position.

'They asked me about three humans,' replied Tangiia, 'two male and one female, and asked if I have seen you. When I ask them "what for?" they tell me both men murder one Soal each and break Soal Law.'

I nodded at Stella, 'Trust Endrod! The Soal Law! He would overstate his case.'

She was about to answer me when Tangiia spoke again.

'This is not why Soal came.'

We both looked at him. Fridjt was shuffling around by the fire throwing more fuel on. An open fire was new to both him and Stella and he was playing with it like a toy. The sudden flaring of the dry grass illuminated Tangiia's face. It carried a puzzled frown.

'Reason, Soal said, is he wants me to help him. He said sky is falling down.'

II

... and the bird-eaters, and those that eat the eaters ...

Journey

I taught Stella how to activate the single brainstinger we found in the chiton.

It was like most Soal innovations, intricate in design and delicate in construction – holding it was like handling a crayfish with long metal legs and the trigger was a hair-thin wire that was activated by the warmth produced between a thumb and fingertip, pressed together. The victim of the weapon's waves was transported instantly into a dream world of demons and succubi that tore open the outer flesh to gain entrance to the inner organs – except that to the victim it was no dream. The brainstinger melted all the walls in the brain between the conscious and sub-conscious.

I taught Stella how to work the weapon but we could not test her skill. It could only be used on a sentient being. Stella liked it.

She also became very fond of the fire – in fact there were times when we literally had to pull her away from it.

'It's clean and bright,' she told me incessantly. Why the fetish with cleanliness I had no idea. I saw no harm in a little filth. Sometimes Stella washed and swam so much I could hardly smell her, and that was not conducive to a good sexual atmosphere.

She did all our cooking for us (another excuse to fondle the flames) and made some superb dishes from the local fish and fruit which Tangiia introduced us to. We had breadfruit and yams and several new types of shellfish. Tangiia told us that if we went collecting ourselves we should avoid the cones, for some of them were poisonous. The textile cone, for example, had a barb harbouring a poison which could be lethal.

All in all our new environment was pleasing, but I feared it was only a matter of time before we were caught. So I resolved to make the best of the time I did have and fill my life with the fruits of enjoyment. This was not a good idea as far as the other two men were concerned, for Stella reserved herself for me alone and would not let either of them touch her. Naturally they became edgy and dispirited and Fridjt never failed to do me some physical annoyance when Stella's back was turned. I of course replied with a verbal attack, but the whole situation began to turn sour on us. Finally I decided something had to be done, mainly because Tangiia was keeping me awake all hours of the night telling me mournful stories of some girl or woman he had once loved – he thought it was quite in order to wake me from a deep sleep to relate a sorrowful tale that he had already told me a dozen times previously. After walking the long, lonely shallows one evening I went back to the clearing to make a sacrifice and approached Stella with a proposition.

As I entered the patch of jungle which Tangiia had cut especially for the hut he had built for Stella (hoping, I suppose, for a return favour), she was bending over the fire turning a spitted fish that Fridjt had trapped in one of his snares. Tangiia was sitting behind her, a few metres away, rigidly regarding her brown, smooth buttocks. The main problem was in full view.

'Stella,' I began as I trod the grass towards her, 'we've got to do something for the other two men.'

She turned and cocked a bushy eyebrow.

'In what way?'

'Well,' I was trying my best to be casual but Tangiia had already perked up and was looking at us intently and I was thankful that Fridjt was nowhere around, 'not *us* exactly, but *you*. They need a woman. I think you ought to give them what they want, what they *need* – occasionally – when I'm not around.'

She snorted.

'*You* give them what they want! I don't like them – not for that anyway.'

Tangiia's head sunk between his knees again and I tried not to look at him.

'Don't be foolish,' I pleaded. 'You can't be *that* averse to it – I mean you once had sex with Fridjt.'

'Fridjt once had sex with me, which is an entirely different matter. The fact that I chose to let him do that, rather than punch my face did not mean I enjoyed it. However,' she lowered her voice placatingly as I began to wind up my fury against Fridjt, 'it's all over and finished with. We have a problem, but the answer doesn't lie with me. It lies with them.' She pointed towards half their number, which was all that was present.

Tangiia smiled broadly. 'You mean we should go and get woman each?' he shouted, astounding me by his quick grasp of things.

'That's exactly it,' answered Stella. 'The sooner the better. We shall all be happier for it.'

Suddenly Tangiia leapt to his feet and began running, down towards his canoe. It took me a few seconds to realize that he was on his way.

'Wait!' I called, running after him. 'Tangiia, wait. Fridjt will want to come too.'

He paused on the sands.

'No room,' he said as I caught up to him. The sand was still hot from the day and I had to keep changing feet in a kind of ritual dance to prevent them from burning.

'Only small canoe. Only room enough for me and,' he grinned, 'two females maybe?'

My hopping was amusing him but I felt I had to make sure he would not leave Fridjt without a woman.

'How will you manage to bring two?'

He nodded and winked.

'I bring two, don't worry,' he replied in that deep resonant voice I envied.

'Two strong hands,' he showed me his opened scarred palms and fingers, then closed them as if gripping hair, 'two females. I will bring them back – you will see.'

'Not *too* young,' I said nervously.

'Who needs children?' he tossed his head at me contemptuously as he turned and dragged his canoe down the sand to the edge of the island. The water was low, and would not be up for some time so I tried to persuade him to wait, but he was too eager. He pushed it out towards the reef into the foam, and swam after the outrigger canoe. His mating canoe.

On impulse I ran after him, I didn't know why – perhaps it was the thought of riding high in that splinter of a boat that appealed to me? Or was I running away from something? It did not matter – the main thing was I knew I wanted to go.

Tangiia tried to prise my hand away from the canoe as it bobbed up and down in the surf.

'One of the women will have another boat,' I said. 'Please let me come?'

He stared for a moment. 'We may be gone long time.'

'It doesn't matter,' I insisted.

He shrugged. 'If you die, you die. She will hate me,' he nodded back towards the camp. 'Maybe. But I don't care about that. Come.'

With that I scrambled aboard and Tangiia ran the Satawal out, leaping inside when it was near the reef. We rode over the top as if we were as light as the breeze which carried us.

I watched the shoreline until it was a black grin on the vast blue ocean and then I turned and talked to Tangiia to hide the fear I felt at leaving firm ground behind and courting the dangers of the open sea.

'Have you thought,' I said to him, 'what a useful weapon fire would be against the Soal? They cannot abide any sudden change in temperature. Stella wants a rebellion. Perhaps we could find some way of using fire.'

I thought about it for a few moments but realized that the reason I liked the idea so much was because it was a weapon that was remote from the user.

'If I were practical,' I continued, 'I should have to admit that the only sure method is to attack the roots of their existence – the mushroom towers. Destroy one of those and the thermostatic balance over the whole world would be upset. Of course, the whole idea is insane,' I added regretfully. 'We have nothing with which we could cause damage.'

Tangiia stared ahead but said, 'Is that why they are so worried about Ostraylean mushroom? Why they want me and other islanders to help in repairing damage?'

'Probably. The Ostraylean tower has always had trouble with subsidence.'

Tangiia paused and idly wiped some seawater from his face while looking in the direction of the great Ostraylean mushroom. There were many such towers scattered around the world but none so large as the one that rose from the north-eastern area of the island continent, up into the banks of cloud above the Earth's surface. This monster was the thermostat for the whole of the south ocean.

'If we could only cause that tower to fall,' I murmured. 'But one of its girders is as wide as a needle tower. It would take more than a handful of humans to move that monster.'

I fell silent then and allowed Tangiia to manage the outrigger without interruption. It was a pleasure to watch him and I felt very envious of his skill. He was a man, complete and able – confident in himself, and he needed no one else, as I did, to lean upon for support. For all his lack of intelligence – and even that fact might only have been a product of my pride, which would not allow me to believe *anyone* was as clever as myself – he could stand alone. He needed motivating, however, otherwise he would have fetched himself a woman on his own initiative.

'You know she will be very angry with you?'

He meant Stella, of course, and I nodded.

'You don't need to go back,' he added. 'There are thousands of islands in my ocean. You can stay away.'

I shook my head.

'No,' I said. I needed Stella, whatever she might lead me into. Then I asked him a question.

'Why haven't you found yourself a woman before this? Surely everyone does not obey the law to the letter? In fact,' I added, 'I seem to be the only human on this earth who does take the law seriously. It appears to be quite normal for young men to slip out into the night to seek comfort in a woman's arms.'

'This may be true,' replied Tangiia, 'but I do not like all women. Most of them live some way from my island – and I want only one woman – she is ... special to me only. Do you understand? I would have gone for her anyway – one day.'

Tangiia had some palm leaves spread on the floor of the canoe and I began to arrange them on top of me. Partly because it would keep the sun off me the following morning and partly to hide me from prying Soal eyes, should a chiton find its way over us. It was not foolproof – but then nothing was that.

'I understand,' I said wearily, falling off to sleep. It only occurred to me as I started to doze that I might offer to help the tan-skinned sailor – perhaps take a shift in the night – but his golden statue in the dying light faded from my mind as I drifted off without speaking.

12

... each like a wave climbing over a wave ...

Wave

Polynesian navigation is legendary. Legends based on historical fact. In the early times, long before the Soal arrived, migrating Polynesian fleets carried with them navigators higher in rank even than their kings. Tangiia was aware of only small excerpts of these old stories but he carried in his frame an inherent aptitude for crossing the wide waters of his ocean. It was an inborn skill that had survived a period of high civilization, though it was necessary to couple natural talent with knowledge. The latter had been retained by the fishermen and adventurers, and Tangiia's ancestor, at the time the Soal arrived, survived because of it.

Legends are stories of adversity dressed in the mysticism of age and the beauty of fine words.

One legend tells that the *Fafakitani*, the Feelers of the Sea, were born on a voyage from Samoa to Tonga when King Taufa'ahau's catamaran-style canoes lost their way. The chief navigators had confessed their ignorance of their location on the wide blue waters when a blind old man, a navigator of low rank, dipped a hand into the sea.

'Tell the King we are in Fijian waters,' he announced after touching the waves.

The chief navigators scoffed but the stores were low and the King asked for more information. He was told by the blind old man, Kaho, that when the sun was in the middle of the sky the flotilla would sight land. A few hours later the fleet arrived at a group of islands to the east of Fiji. Kaho was a hero.

It is said that Kaho confessed many months later to having

been informed of the presence of a fish-eating bird that never ventured far from land – but the Feelers of the Sea did not lose their prestige.

The islands of Tangiia's ocean were green stars flashing on a convex watery sky. Imbedded in millions of square kilometres of sea, they glittered like the scattered fragments of epidote crystals in the morning light. Tangiia paused at the first island with rich growth tumbling down to the beaches that he came across, to take on stores of yams, breadfruit and *nyali* nuts and wrapped them in *pandanus* leaves. Our meat would come from the sea in the form of fish. The boat was already stocked with drinking coconuts.

He was careful not to disturb the undergrowth as he collected his foodstuffs – we did not wish to arouse any occupant of the island. A fight was not what we sought on this journey.

Once on the ocean again he took his course from the wind and current. He was bound he said for Raiatea, where he knew he would find Peloa, the lava-tongued young partner of his recent mating. The spear and the deep narrow target would again find each other out. (*Is it the spear that finds the mark? Or is it the magnetic cleft that draws the spear towards its deep centre?*)

The wind chased the large canoe across the surface of the water leaving transient snail-silver tracks in the waves. Tangiia travelled the paths of his forefathers, using the stars by night and the swells by day, fearfully sniffing the air for 'the stink of ghosts' as he passed an island which had become a nightmare via the tongues of parents who demanded their young's obedience.

Nocturnally he landed to replenish our stores and he skirted the beaches, sometimes to be stared at by aggressive males ready to defend their territories; at other times watched coolly by mothers and young maidens. Once or twice we were tempted by light brown torsos with long black hair, but we resisted, each remembering the dampness of a particular pair of slim young thighs. Better the delight you know than the promise you do not.

At the steering oar hour by hour, for I now took an active part in the sailing, our skins became windburnt and our lips chapped with continual onslaughts from salt water and sun. The small creases round my eyes cracked at the seams to turn to thin red sores and I played my tongue incessantly around the corners of my mouth, making a masochistic game out of the stinging pain, to relieve the boredom. Occasionally Tangiia took down the sail and stretched his body to remove ache from the muscles, before diving into the sea for real physical exercise. I really hated him for being able to swim while I could not. The water looked as inviting as any pleasure I had known. However, he persuaded me that it was safe to climb overboard while he was in the canoe and hang onto the side, allowing my body to float on the sea. After that I did not dislike him so much for being such an athlete.

There was another reason for his fanatical fitness programme. The fact that Peloa might not be alone had occurred to him and he needed to be fit for battle. Polynesians, like anyone else, would not risk death for their prime pleasures.

The training swims were a mixture of flurry and caution. Flurry because Tangiia was not a good swimmer and tended to thrash the water rather than to stroke it, and caution because we both had a healthy respect for sharks and barracuda. The effect desired was achieved in any case: the young man kept his strength, and felt refreshed and revitalized, and I relieved the soreness of my skin.

Afterwards we lay on the smooth, worn wood of his canoe, and he stroked the place where he and Peloa had united in ecstasy, telling me how they created rainbows of passion in each other's minds. She would be pleased to see him, he was sure. She had whispered the words of love in his ear.

Tangiia's home island was Fakaofu, in the Tokelan Islands, more than a thousand kilometres from Peloa's Raiatea. Winds were only ever light because of the small variation in temperature. It would take a very long time to reach her.

One morning, early, we had one of those terrible electrical storms which frightened Stella so much.

As usual the mushroom towers seemed to be taking the brunt of the discharges. We could see two towers from the boat that day, and they seemed to draw in the web of fire as if it were their breath of life. This was a false impression, I know, for it was basic knowledge that the towers provided an earth for the static. Still, it was impressive just the same.

'Look, towers are sending their lines of white fire to one another,' said Tangiia seriously. I chuckled at his ignorance – this was another human misconception and it was easy to see how it came about. The flash was in the sky for less than a split second and it was impossible to ascertain, visually, whether it came from, or went into, the towers. However, my education from the Soal told me that straight, silent lightning came from the same sources as the kind that is accompanied by thunder, which is often seen as a short jagged crack in the sky. Straight lightning storms, which formed their particular concave, tight-knit webs high above the smaller thunder cloud storms, were silent because they took place so high above the atmosphere. We only saw two meteors burn up in the storm – then it was over.

After the storm I tried to explain about the lightning to Tangiia but he was more interested in my life style before I had come to his island, so I ended up by telling him a few stories about life amongst the Soal. He loved it. We were good companions, he and I, and I began to wonder why the humans stayed apart and alone (except for the occasional foray into another's territory to sate sexual needs) for we had come together like magnets, reluctant ever to be parted again. Why hadn't we killed one another, as the Soal taught?

'Humans,' Lintar had once informed me, 'are solitary beasts. They live apart from each other because they react violently to one another's moods. Put two in a cage together and before the month is out one or both will lie dead on the cage floor.' I had believed him then, but I did so no longer. Far from being solitary animals we thrived on one another's companionship. It strengthened us, created confidence and a feeling of security. We could share our fears, and in doing so lessen the effect of those terrors on our minds.

'Shall we get there soon?' I asked Tangiia, who was staring soulfully at the moon, which led me to believe we were quite close to our goal.

He moved his hand on the tiller, slightly changing the course of the canoe, and then answered.

'Not long now. I shall try to reach the beach during the night. If we arrive too early, we'll sail around until it is time to find my woman.'

The prow of our Satawal was alive with phosphorus from the water and pieces of silver water slid along the sides of the boat.

'How do you find your way?' I asked, more to keep him from mournful reflection than anything else. I was enjoying the peace of a night upon calm waters. A warm night. I dangled my fingers in the water, running them through liquid silver.

'I feel big wave and watch for *kaveinga* – stars that make a line for me to follow, see, I will show you.'

He pointed to a star on the horizon and I followed it on its slow journey upwards, until it was high in the night – and then, another star was rising to take its place.

'That's wonderful,' I breathed. 'But I cannot feel the big wave. You must tell me when it next comes so that I can concentrate.'

'I will tell you,' he answered. 'But you must take your hand from water though – there are fish that would eat it. Old word is *mano* – you would say shark.' He grinned at me as I jerked my hand quickly from the water, suddenly remembering that below our idyllic night, under the wavelets, roamed a multitude of grotesque and dangerous monsters. I had been lulled into offering my arm as bait.

'How many old words do you remember Tangiia?' I asked. 'Very many?'

He thought for a while.

'Mostly words of the sea,' he answered finally. 'The navigator's words and those of some fish.'

'Tell me some more.'

He chuckled. 'Some you would find very funny. Perhaps that is why we remember them. I find them beautiful.'

'Such as?'

'There is fish we call *humuhumu-nukunuku-a-puaa.*'

'I don't think that's funny at all,' I said. The word was like music. It sang the name. 'I think it is beautiful too. What does it look like?'

'It looks like this,' he said, letting go of the tiller, and in the moonlight covering his eyes with his hands and peeking through his fingers looking as though he had patches on his cheeks. I laughed.

'And he looks like he is all head, with no body, and when you take him from water, he grunts like this,' and Tangiia then made the most appalling noises.

I laughed again until my chapped lips hurt me too much to continue.

Over the next few hours Tangiia kept repeating that it was 'all so beautiful' and made me feel guilty, because we, Stella and I, had arrived to disrupt his life and possibly take him away from his island to be killed. But then I asked him one evening:

'Would you think everything was so good if Peloa was not alive?'

'No. She is what makes it so beautiful,' he smiled as he spoke. 'Man was made to have woman by his side, otherwise there are just empty holes in our chests where our hearts should be.' I grinned with him.

'Bit of a poet on the sly, aren't you Tangiia? Well, I still can't feel that wave of yours. Tell me again when it comes.'

And so it was over the whole journey. Not all of it was pleasant and I was sick many times. I also found the glaring sun a trial, but we stopped many times on small islands to replenish our store of drinking coconuts and food. In all the journey we did not see one Soal craft, and that worried me. However, Tangiia did not seem to notice their absence so I took it that it was normal for this part of the world.

13

... the Soal shall find these green planets ...

Peloa

It was a moonlit night when we pulled the Satawal canoe towards some bushes that were poised with spidery legs at the water's edge, as if about to step gingerly into the tiny waves.

Slowly and carefully we dragged the craft along the sand and some noise was inevitable as the canoe was heavy, but Tangiia did not wish to leave the craft moored at the water's edge. It would take him time to launch the canoe but the risk of having his beautiful possession stolen was not worth the extra few minutes it would take to refloat it.

Once he was satisfied it was well hidden with palm leaves I followed him cautiously down the shoreline, keeping close to the foliage and trying to avoid the hermit crabs that covered the sand during the dark hours, for their shells crunched loudly beneath bare feet, and also I had no wish to step on a comb shell, with its rows of sharp spikes. We had not been walking long before we could smell wood smoke. Tangiia put a finger to his lips.

Following our noses, and eventually the light of a fire, we crept up to within three metres of the flames. Seated by the blaze, eating a delicious-smelling piglet's leg was a lonely matron of some five hundred months. She was fat and ugly, but her face had a pleasant look about it – a moon-round face with food-loving eyes.

My first instinct was to jump up, grab her by the throat and threaten to strangle her if she did not tell us on what part of the island Peloa lived. But I realized that Tangiia had not the heart to attack this well-layered, simple woman and instead I suggested in whispers that he frighten her gently into giving him the information. He nodded, then cupping his hands to his mouth he moaned softly.

'Oooah Peloa, who knows where you are my little angel-fish of seas? This is spirit of her lover calling. If you who sit there...'

He had no time to finish for the fat woman was on her feet and streaking away from the firelight screaming at the top of her voice.

'Keep away, you dirty old man. No more jig-jig with Lipsua. I've got to eat sometime. Keep that thing away from me!'

We realized the situation was far from lawful, and that the fat matron was not lonely at all – at least not most of the time – and Tangiia rose and bounded after her, flung his arms around her chest and grabbed her huge bouncing breasts. She struggled, mouthing oaths while he tried to calm her.

'Off me, you ...' Suddenly she stopped wriggling, realizing that the arms that bound her were not the usual stringy, wrinkled limbs that grappled for her ample melons.

'Oh, that's nice. That's very good,' she giggled, ceasing all attempts at freeing herself and starting to stroke Tangiia's thick-muscled left thigh.

'Stop that,' he growled. I could see he was beginning to become aroused in spite of her ugliness. It was, after all, a long time since the last mating.

'You want me?' she crooned. 'See I don't struggle any more. I help you do it, yes?'

'No. I'm looking for girl. Girl named Peloa. She is young, with long black hair down to here.' He let her go and she turned, hands on hips to appraise him in the firelight.

'First we do it. Then you can look for this girl, yes?' she said hopefully.

Tangiia glared at her, beginning to lose his patience. He un-hooked his war club from the cord around his middle and threatened her with it.

'You must tell me quickly, or I will bust your brains like coconut, you fat old sow.'

'No need for insults,' she sniffed, unimpressed by his aggressiveness.

'I've got a man too. If I call him he'll come running to smash you to pieces.' She ran her eyes contemptuously up and down Tangiia's tall frame.

'He's bigger than you,' she lied feebly.

Tangiia began to get desperate. Hiding in the bushes I thought about paddling her backside with the club but realized that violence would only alienate her. However, it seemed Tangiia had an idea.

'How would you like man that is really bigger than me?'

The mound of fat quivered.

'Bigger than you?' she asked her eyes opening wide.

Tangiia nodded, smiling.

I hoped he was sacrificing Fridjt to this quivering mound of flesh and not me. She would suffocate a man my size with affection.

'You can come out Cave,' called Tangiia.

I sheepishly stepped out from the cover of the bushes into the light of the fire.

'This is not *big* man,' she said indignantly.

'Not him,' answered Tangiia. 'Another man, on another island.'

She seemed mollified for the moment and began describing a young girl that lived on the far side of the island. Tangiia nodded in excitement, exclaiming, 'Yes, yes! That's Peloa. That's the girl I came for. Take us to her.'

The fat woman led the way along a dark jungle path that had me stumbling along behind the sure-footed natives. Trees and vines are not the best landmarks either and I was anxious in case this woman ran off and left us stranded in the dense foliage. Finally we reached a clearing, in the centre of which was a small hut of palm leaves. Tangiia immediately rushed forward and blundered into the hut calling, 'Peloa! Peloa!'

I groaned. He was sure to frighten the girl badly that way. The woman and I waited outside and listened.

After a short spell of silence there was a moan : the sound of someone waking from a deep sleep; and then a question.

'Me, Tangiia. You remember your lover?' was the soft reply.

Another silence, then a spitting sound and an ugly word. I heard a female voice say, 'I am too young.'

Perplexed, I turned to the woman.

'Do you know what is happening in there?' I asked.

She nodded but declined to tell me the secret, turning back to the hut. Sounds of an animal trapped in undergrowth then.

There was a yell and then Tangiia came out of the hut with a grim expression on his face. He was dragging a small girl, plump as a pigeon, by both her wrists. As soon as he let go of her she tried to rake his chest with her nails. Desperately he grabbed at the wrists, missing one of them. The girl screamed abuse at him and flailed him with her free hand about the head and ears. Finally, after some minutes had elapsed, she fell sobbing to her knees. Tangiia still held her and he lifted her up gently in his arms, carrying her towards the path.

'Well?' I asked him as he passed. He did not even look at me and I tagged on behind the trio of Polynesians, all sharing a secret which was denied me. I felt an outsider.

Tangiia did not, as he promised, take the fat woman with us. He pushed her away roughly as she tried to climb into the already overcrowded canoe. She protested, and so did I, but we could all see that it would be an impossible journey with all four of us. I felt he was quite wrong to have promised her anything in the first place – but I had to admit to him later that she did have her own canoe and had she been desperate to follow us she could have set out in that while our sail was still in sight. At least the girl Peloa was calm at last and I tended the tiller, looking at the stars, the sea, anywhere except at the two lovers who caressed each other beneath my precious palm leaves.

Fishing with a line has a magical quality about it that is difficult to describe. It is a man's physical connection with the unknown, an extension of him reaching into another, a supernatural, world in which the environment is hostile to his body. Mystery and horror lurked in the depths.

I sat in the bows of the canoe with the taut line between my fingers trying to imagine what was going on beneath the surface and waiting for the jerk that would set my heart racing with excitement. Tiptihani was completely managing our tiller – I was inclined to think that she was even more skilful than Tangiia, who was about a hundred metres to starboard.

Tiptihani was Peloa's mother but she had given birth to Peloa when she was still very young and was now a mature but extremely handsome woman: a square but feminine jawline was held high, and a beautiful skin shone golden in the sunlight. I studied her hair that was too heavy to be lifted by the light breeze which carried us along. It was thick and black, and it fell to her waist eclipsing the tanned breasts that were still high and firm. We had called at Tiptihani's island on the insistence of Peloa and had persuaded the girl's mother to accompany us to Tangiia's home. It was her canoe that carried me and my line across the placid surface of the sea.

'Why do you stare at me?' she asked, turning slowly so that the eclipse was over for one of the orbs.

'I'm sorry,' I said, my eyes riveted in spite of her obvious discomfort. 'I was just dreaming – thinking about something. It's very pleasant just to lie here in the sun and dream.'

She nodded. 'It's pleasant to dream – so long as dreams are not too ...'

'Ambitious?' I finished for her. She was warning me off.

Suddenly the line almost cut my fingers off and I gave a yell of excitement and pain that turned the heads of Peloa and Tangiia. Tangiia smiled when he saw me feverishly pulling in the line, and waved.

It was a reddish-coloured fish with a hard bony mouth that I finally landed flapping in the Satawal. It disappointed me. I had expected it to be much larger, judging by the strength of the pull. But it was still a fish – and I had caught it. I dangled it proudly before Tiptihani.

'Pretty good eh? I didn't realize I was so skilful at this sort of thing.'

Tiptihani smiled. 'Sea is full of fish and they are always hungry.'

A bit crestfallen I said, 'Yes, I suppose it's not such a brilliant feat – still, it means we can eat,' I added with a little more heart in the words.

I took out a knife, slit the fish open and began slicing slivers of raw flesh from it. These I put on chunks of coconut and handed them one at a time to Tiptihani, at the same time popping one or two into my own mouth. They were quite tasty, but then one's taste varies with the circumstances.

A few weeks ago, when we had all the cooked pork we could eat, I would not have looked twice at raw fish. It is not only hunger that makes one appreciate such simple dishes : it is also the state of one's body and mind. I was beginning to feel strong. Sailing over a sun-hammered ocean for week upon week had forged my body into a hardness that would not have seemed possible while I was living amongst the Soal. I was no longer a frail, pallid creature full of indecision. My body was brown, wiry and in a constant state of exhilaration. The white salt found creases that had not been there before the trip – creases that had formed at the lower contours of knotted muscles. I moved with the sureness and swiftness necessary to control a small boat. Tangiia was not always softly spoken and kindly – at moments when the canoe needed two competent pairs of hands he bawled orders that had to be obeyed accurately and quickly, otherwise stinging remarks about my origins followed rapidly behind. The crowning indignity was when he pushed me roughly out of the way and did the job himself. I don't think I ever wished for anything in my life as much as I wanted praise from Tangiia after one of those flurries when we gybed or came about to avoid a hidden reef. When it finally came I felt as a hawk must feel the first time he makes a stoop and kills. No one was as full of pride as I was.

'Tiptihani?' I questioned the silent woman, 'Why was Peloa so upset when Tangiia first found her? Has he hurt her in some way?'

Tiptihani smiled wryly.

'My daughter is having child,' she answered. 'It is probably my fault that she dislikes this idea. I never wanted child so young, especially girl. I wanted excitement and adventure and baby needs constant attention. As girl child grows older it needs protecting from men. If girl is too young at mating it can do her harm.' She paused and looked out across the water.

'I suppose I often grumbled about this to Peloa when she was small and it has given her set views.'

'I see,' I replied, and considered this fact – that one person might impress another with his or her opinions. This was why

Stella and I were so incompatible. Her former lifestyle was so different from my own. Not a very brilliant deduction but then I had only just learned to think for myself.

It was as I was thinking to myself that I saw a fish break water a long way off, and then return to the deeps. A porpoise? What exactly was it that I had seen? I asked myself. A flash? Porpoises do not usually flash silver. They are brown-backed and slide serpentine when they surface. Besides, the flash that had caught my eyes was brilliant – like the flashing of a mirror. Or glass. Something highly polished.

It hit me then.

'Tiptihani,' I said. 'I don't want to alarm you but we're being followed by a Soal craft.'

It was the wrong thing to have said. Her face immediately registered fright.

'Don't tell the others,' I warned. 'Peloa will only panic and in their small boat it could be disastrous. Especially since she's pregnant.'

This had the right effect and the woman nodded with a slightly calmer expression.

'Can we do anything?'

'Nothing. We'll just have to wait for them to make the first move.'

14

... shall wash over them and the life beneath ...

Split

We were not approached by those that were following us and I began to wonder whether my assumption had been correct. Perhaps the flash I had seen *had* been a fish? But the thought was nagging me that we had not seen a single Soal craft while we had been on the ocean and I realized that if the Soal were pursuing us under water they would probably warn all other Soal vehicles away in order that they might continue to follow us and discover the purpose for an unlawful gathering of humans.

After her initial show of fear Tiptihani remained cool and we spoke to each other of our plight only when her daughter and Tangiia were out of earshot.

'If you're right Cave,' she said to me on the third day afterwards, 'when do you think they will come for us?'

'I wish I knew,' I replied. 'As we get closer to Tangiia's island we had better decide where to land. We don't want Stella and the others in the same trouble.'

She saw the obvious logic in this and realized that, however free we were at the moment, there was to be no escape for us. The Soal would eventually rise to the surface and arrest us. It was a dismal prospect but it was one we had to face.

About noon that day we saw a strange sight to the west. It was a cloud, so low that it touched the surface of the sea. I turned in the canoe and narrowed my eyes, trying to find some definition in the shape.

'What's that?' I pointed towards the cloud and even as I was doing so it seemed to expand along the whole horizon, rolling like a high wave along the surface of the sea.

Tiptihani shrugged. 'I don't know. Shall I call to Tangiia?'

But Tangiia had already seen it himself and he was looking as puzzled as we were. Inspecting it closer I could see dark patches running through the cloud as it swept over the water towards us.

'Perhaps we can lose the Soal inside there, whatever it is?' said Tiptihani hopefully.

'I don't think that's possible,' I replied. 'They're using non-visual means to keep us under surveillance. The cloud will make no difference.'

'What?'

'It doesn't matter,' I said. 'We can't avoid them, that's all.'

By this time the cloud was almost upon us and I could hear thunder in the distance. Tangiia shouted something, standing up in his canoe, and then we were swallowed by the cloud.

Within seconds we were soaking wet and covered in grime. It was warm inside the cloud and I realized what it was – steam mixed with dust and ash. We did have a chance, I thought, because though the Soal could surface in the cloud, they would not be able to leave their vehicle unless they had thermosuits with them. It was not normal to carry thermosuits on routine patrol. They could still follow us of course, but only *one* of us. The other boat could escape.

I deliberately turned the Satawal to windward and towards the source of the steam and soot. Tiptihani watched the action with some apprehension.

'Cave?' she said in a frightened voice.

'The Soal can only follow one of us,' I explained. 'If it's our boat, well then we've still got a chance if we can get to the place where this vapour is coming from. I don't know about you but the only explanation I can think of is a volcano . . .'

She confirmed my thoughts.

'Yes, they won't come too near an eruption – but what if there're two of them? Or even more?'

'We haven't got a lot of choice have we? If Weyym's kind to us there won't be any Soal at all, but I'm afraid my faith hasn't been all it should be lately.'

Black flecks were settling and sticking to our wet skins. Occasionally it was a hot piece and sharp spots of pain kept me cursing and attentive to my task. Having to beat to windward was a time-consuming activity – but then we had all the time we needed. The Soal were certainly not going to surface in the steam and ash.

We kept up our tacking for about an hour at the end of which I was running with rivulets of grime, and there was still no sign of the source of the activity, though we could hear the explosions and the sizzling of hot rock touching water. It only occurred to me when we were obviously close to the place where the earth was disgorging its viscous bile that we might be in danger. At any moment a heave from the belly of the world might end our lives.

Feeling my way carefully, I lowered the sail and allowed the canoe to drift. We could hear the fall of surf to port now but it was difficult to tell if the noise was a reef or some other natural musician. Whatever it was I had no desire to slam into it at full speed.

Suddenly we were out of the steam cloud and back into bright sunlight. There was still a lot of dust in the air but we had come out to the far side of the island that owned the volcano. It was still spitting and coughing up its igneous coke but the volcano itself was in the centre of the island and its strength was beginning to flag and the ash was not now reaching the shoreline.

There were fires everywhere and at first I thought it might be a completely new island: then I saw patches of green amongst the black and realized that what had once been jungle was now buried beneath layers of new rock. We paddled around the lagoon after skipping over the reef and found a spot on the beach that was protected by an overhanging rock. I ran the canoe onto this spot and we tumbled out to lie on the cinder-flecked sand by a charred stump that not long ago had been a tree. Smouldering, it jutted aggressively from the ground like a master torturer's favourite toy.

'Well, we're here,' I said. 'Still alive and kicking.'

I turned to look at the Polynesian woman as she rolled over on her back. A half-dead fruit bat lay amongst the debris not far from her. It was flapping a holed wing in its agony so I climbed to my feet, stepped gingerly over the warm ash and trod on it quickly. Weyym knows how many other poor creatures were suffering a similar fate on the island – or were already dead.

As I passed by Tiptihani again, she took hold of my ankle and on gaining my attention pointed out to sea. Coming around the corner of the reef, obviously searching for the moving craft that had disappeared from the viewer, was a half visible Soal craft. It dived beneath the waves a second later having seen the canoe and we were left in no doubt as to our position. We stayed where we were because there was nowhere else to run to, and we let the day move rapidly into sunset without moving – one of the most bloody-eyed dusks I have ever witnessed, and soon the only light was that of the torch that flamed from the cone behind us.

Tiptihani moved close to me when the night came and touched me gently. What had aroused her I did not know – it could have been any number of things from a desire to leave the world sating her carnal needs, or merely the excitement of the day's activities. I do know that the mating we had was a slow sensuous experience which changed my whole outlook on sex. Until then my sexual knowledge had consisted entirely of the rabbit-quick matings which satisfied Stella but which left me feeling as if I had been rapidly tried, tested and cast aside for a better model.

Heedless of the ash in our mouths and on our skin we kissed and fondled each other half into the night and even when it was over and I was feeling peaceful and warm inside, I lay in the occulting light of the flares and watched her fall off to sleep. She had passed the age when her beauty was at its height but she had a serene aura about her. Stella was all angles, hollow cheeks and thrusting aggressiveness. Tiptihani was soft and feminine – but at the same time she had a quiet sort of strength that was less evident than Stella's but more deep-rooted and stable. I hoped I would never have to choose between the two women – the prospect was certainly rather unlikely considering our circumstances – because it would be an impossible choice. What I really wanted was a woman that combined the qualities of both Tiptihani and Stella.

I felt her stir and looked down. She was not asleep after all. She was studying me with her large brown eyes.

'You didn't like me,' she stated firmly.

'That's not quite correct,' I replied. 'I liked it very much – you very much – it was just different to what I'm used to that's all. I'm not very sure of myself.'

She nodded.

'That's very true – I felt it. You're not very good with women. Cave – you need good teacher. I could teach you but I like men to be strong with me. I don't like to be strong one.'

I was indignant with her.

'Why do you say that? Didn't I make enough decisions today?'

'Decisions were made for you.'

I did not agree with that view and said so, but she merely turned over and went back to sleep without answering.

After a while I rose carefully to avoid waking her and picked my way using the intermittent patches of light, to the edge of the water. The sea was calm, still and black and just looking at it helped to quell the turbulence in my mind. I was trying to decide what we should do next. Stay where we were? We should soon run out of stores. Sail away again? I had no doubt the Soal would pick us up before we went a hundred metres. Go inland? That seemed the best idea, though there was no guarantee that we would be safer or less hungry there. Still, it was the best of the three choices and it would be interesting if nothing else. I had never seen a volcano before, let alone an active one throwing up fiery bouquets of flowers.

But why hadn't the Soal come for us? I hoped there was something about the volcano or the island that was keeping them away.

15

... this is the way of life within the form that is me ...

Squares

The lava flow had found its way down the west lip of the volcano and had reached the sea, forming a promontory out into the lagoon. It was this that had caused the steam. Those parts that were cool enough to walk upon were extremely sharp where blisters had burst and solidified and we decided that however much the occasional patches of cinders burnt the soles of our feet we would stick to walking on the ash.

Both Tiptihani and I were refreshed after the night's rest and our sea legs had adjusted to solid ground. Early in the morning we had washed in the murky water and had begun to climb over the foothills towards the edge of the volcano. Soot was still spasmodically puffing out of the vent and the groaning and creaking of cooling rock assailed our ears from all directions, but the low growling of under-earth activity had ceased – at least for the time being. Clouds hung above the gaping mouth making it seem as though the mountain was about to swallow them as they swirled above it and I was reminded of a prehistoric beast come to life for a few moments and then freezing in action. The image pleased me because volcanoes are themselves archaic links with an unreachable past. There was one person, a certain Soal librarian, that I would have gladly sacrificed and fed to the monster.

'What're you thinking of?' asked Tiptihani, pausing for breath. 'You looked so vicious.'

I realized I was snarling and immediately turned it into a laugh.

'I was thinking of roasting a Soal in the fires of that mouth ahead.'

'Why?'

'Because he killed my father, that's why. Anyway, it's not important at the moment.'

I looked around the dreary landscape. Palm trees with no heads, or at the least with very singed tops, poked through waves of grey dust. There were still one or two small fires burning but the soot had suffocated most of the naked flame.

'Not a very pretty place is it?' I said. 'A few days ago this was as beautiful as the island you just left.'

My eyes continued to sweep the ground ahead. We were in a small valley at the end of which I could see a pool. The pool was being filled by a long, thin waterfall – the tail of a stream that had its origins on the higher slopes. It was a peculiar colour but at least it was fresh water. We could filter it through grass – if we could find some grass.

We made our way towards the pool which, like our spot on the beach, had been partly saved by the overhanging brow of rock that dribbled the stream. Tiptihani suggested that we used her hair to filter the water, which seemed like a good idea, but as we got closer we could see that it would not be necessary – the water was reasonably clear, and it was only around the spot where the waterfall struck the surface that it was cloudy.

One or two birds were drinking as we approached, which was a good sign. If they were returning, the situation must seem almost normal. Animals and birds have a far keener instinct for normality than civilized man.

We fell to our knees at the edge of the fresh water and took in long draughts. My throat was parched from the walk and though we carried drinking coconuts we were not sure how long we had to make them last. It was when I raised my head from the last pull, to wipe my mouth and beard, that I caught sight of something beside the waterfall. It was a shape – a symmetrical positioning of wooden poles and posts, and I realized at once that it must have been made by an intelligent being.

'What's that?' I said to Tiptihani.

She looked up and squinted with her eyes at the shape, some twenty square metres in area.

'I don't know.'

We climbed to our feet and walked towards it. I wondered if it had any religious meaning – perhaps the area inside the arrangement of poles was sacred. There were three sets of poles, some of which were damaged or broken, arranged horizontally one on top of the other with a space of thirty centimetres between them. These were fixed to upright posts and arranged to form a roughly-shaped square.

'Look at this,' said Tiptihani, brushing some ash away from the bottom layer. Stuck between the ground and the first pole was the skeleton of an animal.

'What is it?' I asked her.

'Wild pig,' she replied, 'but see – it's on inside of poles. Trying to get out it must have jammed fast and starved to death. Poor creature.'

'Very strange,' I said. 'How do you think it got in there?'

'Perhaps Polynesian man kept him for fresh meat?'

I looked at her sceptically. Why keep a pig when there were plenty running around in the forest? Besides, I had noticed that Tangiia ate mostly fish – that was his life, fishing.

'Maybe,' I answered, but more to avoid argument than in actual agreement. I touched the top pole and it crumbled. The wood was beginning to rot.

'Let's see what else we can find?'

We rummaged around for a while and Tiptihani made the next discovery: an old clay pot, but this one, in comparison with others I had seen amongst the Polynesians, was finely made with a smooth exterior. The owner had obviously turned it on a machine and probably used a hot fissure in the volcano as a kiln to fire it.

We kept the pot for our own use and walked on up the valley, finally coming to the dwelling of the human at the end. Unlike the grass and palm huts of the Polynesians it was a solid construction built of dry stone and whoever was inside must have been protected from the falling ash, which lay about fifty centimetres thick over the ground. Here was a true artisan and one I was now longing to meet.

'Careful,' remarked Tiptihani, hanging back. 'I don't like this place.'

I laughed at her.

'Don't be silly, woman. After an experience like this man has gone through he will be glad someone has entered his territory. You forget – we're being chased anyway. This man might know of somewhere to hide.'

When I looked however the inside was so dark and gloomy I could make out nothing. Not a thing stirred when I called tentatively into the interior. Finally, realizing the place was empty, I stepped boldly through the rugged stone doorway and allowed my eyes to become used to the light. They eventually did so, and when they became adjusted the nape of my neck crawled with insects. It was sitting upright, glaring straight at me.

I jumped outside gagging with fright, at the same time telling myself not to be so stupid. It was only a body after all. A spider came dashing through the doorway and between my legs.

Tiptihani was almost ready to run herself.

'Is he in there?' she called from several metres away.

'She,' I corrected. 'Yes, she's there but she's harmless. It's only a corpse – pretty far gone by the look of it too.'

I went inside again and stared at the old woman – she must have been old, the hair hung white and lank from the skull. She was sitting on some sort of square wooden stool with arms. Whatever the origin of the culture of this human she must have had a fetish for square objects – everything was square, the religious area by the pool, the hut and the chair. Symmetry gone mad. I was fascinated with the corpse though – I had never seen a dead human before, only radioactive dust.

Tiptihani came to the doorway and immediately began backing off again.

'Ugh! Smell!' she exclaimed.

'Smell?' I replied, aware of it for the first time. The visual effect of the woman's body was so stunning I had not noticed the odours before.

'It's horrible,' announced Tiptihani emphatically, but she advanced again, fascinated by my obvious interest in the corpse.

'How long has she been dead?'

'I don't know – two or more months. Look she's covered her body with a blanket or something. I wonder why? Perhaps she had a disease that was ugly to look at, so don't touch her.'

'I wasn't going to,' snorted my companion.

'Look at that!' I cried, pointing to a table in the corner of the hut.

'Another square! I tell you everything this person had was cuboid or square. It's a strange religion which has somehow survived all these thousands of months of alien rule. Perhaps the volcano kept the Soal away from this place and a whole community of humans lived here – this woman perhaps being the last, since no one has moved her body. Let's look around the place some more – perhaps we can find out something else – something that would confirm my conjecture.'

'Perhaps Soal will come and send you to Weyym to find out?' replied Tiptihani. 'Why are we wasting our time around this place – let's go on Cave? We can fill pot from stream.'

I stared at her. She was right of course. We had to move.

'Right,' I replied reluctantly, 'let's go on then – but it's a shame. We might have found the answer to a lot of questions here.'

We left the old woman, where she sat, staring through her doorway at her island home. We continued our climb but on a slope not far from the house we encountered some mounds. Pausing for a few minutes I shovelled away the ash and soft earth with my hands. Whatever it was though, that lay buried beneath, was quite deep and we had no time. There was no doubt in my mind that if I continued to dig, the object that I would eventually uncover would be square or cuboid. It had to be. Everything we had seen so far was, except the pot – and pots are always rounded.

All that day we climbed the volcano and late in the afternoon we reached as far as we could go. The sulphur in the air made our eyes water and our nostrils sting. The ground was piping hot beneath our bare feet and it was difficult to stand still. We stared up at the lip, which still belched the odd breath of gas, and resigned ourselves to the fact that there was no way we could stay up there. We should soon run short of water and though there were still signs of small animal life in amongst the charred tree stumps and occasional green patch, we had no means of catching it.

We began the long walk back down the slopes to the beach far below. I do not know what we hoped to achieve by walking everywhere – perhaps it was a throwback to my mudwalking days when I moved from tower to tower – also without purpose. Humans are restless creatures and when in a state of agitation would rather do something than nothing. To have sat and waited for the Soal would have been unthinkable.

Part of the way down we found a bird, possibly a parrot, that had been caught by the ashes and roasted. It was quite edible towards the middle, and washed down with water taken from the stream, helped to quell the noises issuing from our stomachs. Afterwards the sun began to disappear as quickly and as elegantly as it always did in this corner of the world. Black follows scarlet closely and with great effect.

We curled up with the taste of burnt feathers in our mouths and fell asleep in each other's arms.

16

... and when I shall end, so will all else end ...

Capture

There was a noise. I opened one eye and the light of dawn burned right through to my brain and I had to wait and blink a long time for objects to come into focus. It came again and I swivelled the eyeball, chameleon-wise, rather than move my head, in the direction of the sound. About two hundred metres away a Soal was stealing with a hunched back from one rock to another.

Instantly I was on my feet, pulling Tiptihani with me.

'Run!' I urged her. 'They've caught up with us.'

She struggled along beside me still groggy from her deep sleep. My head was none too good either as the air was still not clear of gases from the vent. We had run headlong down the slope for about four hundred metres when, gasping for breath, she turned and looked upwards.

'Where? Where's their vehicle?'

I stopped. She was right – where was their vehicle? They could not have hidden it on the stark landscape between the top of the volcano and the foothills below. Why should they bother to walk to us?

'There's something just a little bit strange about all this,' I said. 'You keep moving towards that clump of boulders ahead. I'm going to try to see what they're doing.'

Tiptihani did as she was told and I ran swiftly behind a spur of the lava flow, then climbing cautiously on the jagged rock I peered over the corner to see if they were following us.

They were still coming, but very slowly and with elaborate stealth, pausing every so often to look ahead of them.

Weyym's mucus! They were spying on us!

It must have been a long time since the Soal had had to do anything that involved subterfuge and they were not very good at it. They looked like their own children playing games and if the situation had not been so grave I would have found it humorous. The question, among many questions, was why were they doing it? The leader had a brainstinger in his hand and I could see no real reason for not using it.

I climbed down and ran on to where Tiptihani was struggling in a deep area of ash. I pulled her out roughly and we continued skipping over the loose cinders, downwards towards a comparatively large patch of greenery.

'What shall we do?' she asked desperately, as we paused for breath under cover of the bushes. A lizard stood, high on his forelegs, throat pulsing, regarding us from a near-by ledge.

'I don't think we need do anything for a while. They don't seem interested in taking us captive just yet. All they seem to want to do is observe us – without being seen themselves.'

'But we've seen them!'

'Yes, and they know it – but their orders are presumably not to approach us. Do you think we've picked up some sort of disease or something without knowing it? Perhaps they're frightened to come any closer?'

'How could we have done that? We've been at sea last few days and before that on our islands.'

I shook my head.

'Well, see for yourself,' I said, waving my hand towards our enemy. 'They're not coming any closer. Every time we stop, they stop. It's like one of the Soal comedy mimes. I admit the military can be stupid, but they've never acted like this before. They obviously know something of which we're unaware. Come on – let's get down to the beach.'

I rose to continue our journey to the shore.

When we reached the beach some while later we trotted along the shoreline looking for the Satawal. Perhaps we could get out of range before the Soal got back to their subsea craft? I told Tiptihani. It was a very long shot as they would no doubt have left someone in the vehicle.

The Satawal came into sight and I slowed my jog to a walking pace as we drew near to it.

Reaching the canoe Tiptihani immediately jumped in. I intended to follow but my foot dislodged a stone as I prepared to spring – except that it was not a stone, it was a grey, warty fish, and one of its dorsal spines entered my instep. I screamed – high and long. So high in fact, that no sound actually came to my throat.

'Look out!' said Tiptihani as the fish scudded through the shallows and under a stone. 'Don't touch it.'

I paled. 'I already have,' I said hoarsely, for the pain in my foot was making it difficult to breathe.

'Oh no,' she whispered, the colour draining from her face, which frightened me beyond measure.

'What was it?' I cried.

Tiptihani, seeing my distress, immediately regained her composure.

'Don't worry, just sit down quietly and try not to move. That is important. If you move poison will reach your heart much more quickly.'

I could feel my heart pounding in my chest, accelerating with the onrush of panic. Blood thudded in my ears as my head filled with pain and my sight began to fail, the greyness moving in from outside edges of my field of vision. I made a quick, and for me, courageous decision.

'Go on Tiptihani. Leave me here.'

She hesitated, then she said,

'It is best Soal find you – otherwise you will die.' Then she ran away to drop the mainsail and put out to sea. I watched the tall canoe skip the reef before sinking to my knees.

I was getting weaker and more afraid as the moments slipped away from me. I was dying – I felt it. What a useless man I was. I had done nothing of any consequence in my whole life. I groaned aloud. Finally they arrived, just before I dropped down the pit of blackness into unconsciousness.

'Help me,' I managed to beg of my persecutors. I dimly perceived one of them bending over me, and then I let go of the edge of awareness.

The shaft I had fallen into was as deep as Weyym's universe it-self – and while I fell my head spun with fantasies of dinosaurs, crunching in gargantuan pleasure on the brittle bodies of Soal. The Soal had had dinosaur-like creatures in their evolutionary cycle on their old world, but their formative era had overlapped that of the giant lizards and their folk lore was full of dragons, real and created. It had impressed the birdmen to find that Earth had also been trodden flat by tons of reptilian flesh and bone. So I enjoyed the spectacle of monstrous teeth splintering Soal bones, even though my head felt like metal and my stomach was emptying itself, over and over again, like a mountain water-fall throwing forth its contents in spasmodic surges.

I swam to semi-consciousness once or twice before becoming fully aware of my surroundings. The first time I merely sensed a dim green light with figures moving to and fro across it. Then I again drifted off into a dream world. The second time a dis-torted Soal face was inches away from my own. A finger was lifting my eyelid and the owner appeared to be attempting to look inside my head, using my eye as a window. When I finally struggled to the surface for the third time I managed to stay there.

I felt extremely weak and my head was impossible to lift but I was at least still alive. The green light was still with me and I seemed to be sharing my room with some inquisitive fish that swam backward and forwards alongside by bunk. Reaching out I attempted to touch one – and touched the transparent panel between the fish and me instead. I realized where I was then – in a cabin inside the Soal craft, and we were obviously sub-merged and moving slowly.

I tried to raise myself but the effort got me nowhere and only made me feel like vomiting. There were weeds outside, and all the colours of coral that Tangiia had shown me on the island, so we were in very shallow water. Just as I was contemplating this the plants dropped away and the ocean took on a darker hue. We were on our way into deep ocean.

The cabin door opened and a Soal entered. He or she was an elderly alien but not doting.

'Where are we going?' I asked in a voice that surprised even me with its dullness.

The Soal regarded me for a moment and then said in its own language and frequency, 'It is of no use speaking – I don't understand Terran. But I am told you can mouth-read our language so I will tell you some answers to the questions you are probably asking me. The girl is not with us – she has sailed away on her own ...'

I felt guilty for a moment since her welfare had not been my prime concern. I had been worried about my own circumstances.

'... we let her believe in her escape because it will suit a superior's purpose. My name is Reandeller by the way ...' A female name, '... and I have no interest in all this intrigue. I am a doctor, straight and simple, and my one concern is to get you back to health – after which I understand they're going to execute you, but that doesn't interest me either. If the execution goes wrong and you end up a cripple, *then* I shall be interested once more – however, to get back to the task in hand, you are in a craft heading towards Ostraylea and at the moment you are still very ill. It took me some while to analyse the poison and produce an antidote – but, well, you're alive at least. I don't know how much damage has been done to your internal organs but as long as you lie still for a while I don't think there's anything that we can't repair ...'

'And then burn with the rest of me,' I retorted as hotly as my condition would allow, forgetting she could not understand – but she understood my face.

The crossed-beaks from Reandeller.

'Ah,' she said, 'I see that amused you. Well, one can never tell. Tomorrow we may have decided to create an amnesty for all political prisoners and you will be free, and thanks to me, whole and healthy. Who can say? I'll let you sleep now, and be assured that no one ...'

And there the information ended for she had forgotten I was reading and not listening, and had turned towards the door, still speaking. I could have finished it off though '... no one will disturb you until you're well again.' A true Soal, Reandeller. She minded her own business – with her rank and position if necessary.

That left me minding *my* business – and business consisted of very dreary pastimes. I concentrated on watching the ocean smooth by the window. The fish were not numerous and they tended to be of the predator variety – not at all picturesque in appearance but beautiful to watch none-the-less. Muscular sharks and the brown bodies of porpoise in full ... I was thinking of flight, since they resembled birds in their gracefulness. But even new pastimes pall when they are replayed by the day and I gradually sank into gloom and depression.

My depression remained with me even when I regained enough strength to stand and walk about the cabin. Apart from the almost paralysing fear of the certain death I was about to face, haunting me night and day, there was also the agonizing experience of the delay in reaching our destination. I did not want to reach Ostraylea and my execution – but at the same time I was not fool enough to think the craft was heading directly for that place. For one thing we were travelling much too slowly and for another we occasionally paused outside island reefs. I got the impression that the craft was checking other islands using a haphazard route – but I was not sure enough to be satisfied. Waiting to die is a terrifying experience – waiting to begin to wait, and not knowing how long, shreds the spirit.

Reandeller did not ease the situation by visiting me occasionally, for she never failed to leave me puzzling over some enigmatic remark.

'You can forget your friend,' she said one time, 'for he never forgets to remember you.'

If she was being sadistically sarcastic she meant Endrod. If not, Lintar. One of them, I was sure, would be waiting for me at the end of the journey. Since it would make no difference whether I lived or died which one it was, I hoped it would be Endrod. He at least would not be heavily censorious of my actions and at the same time full of pity for me – Endrod would only gloat.

Reandeller also brought me a small fine-meshed wire cage the shape and size of a husked coconut. Inside the cage were two mayflies – she said she bred a multitude of flies as a hobby and to inquire into various ways of spreading bacteria – an activity useful for wiling away submersion time. As I watched the insects delicately picking their way over the wires and joining together in what appeared to be sexual union, Reandeller told me I should be interested because they lived approximately a day, and that short lifetime was spent exploring carefully the inside of a cage.

'It may serve to remind you that your *day* is nearing its end,' she said, 'and the similar explorations you decided to embark upon in your own prison will soon be over. And what will they have taught you? These explorations? The answer is from the two insects – you will learn that you have lived and died in a cage.'

I thought at first she meant my prison was the world, but Soal are usually very precise and she did say 'inside' the cage. I realized, after staring for a whole day at the contours of the mayfly prison with its remarkable resemblance to a human skull, that she didn't mean the globe – she meant my head.

With excellent timing on Reandeller's part, we reached the end of our journey a few moments after the second mayfly died.

17

... my eyes shall hold no more light,
for when the suns have flared ...

Daylong

I was taken in a chiton by the sea captain to a place inland where the main Soal community lay, beneath the shadow of the giant mushroom. All the way there I stared out, first at the coastal green, and then the desert fringes with its patches of jungle encroaching on sand, thinking that this was probably my last view of the outside world.

The one that was waiting my arrival at the Soal-made oasis beside the tower was of course Endrod. He greeted me without malice, but then proceeded to berate the seacraft captain for having arrested me, which he must have done once already, when the craft had reported my capture. The captain stood with averted face while I watched the tirade, not even pretending to understand why the captain was being reprimanded instead of praised for bringing me to justice.

When it was all over Endrod turned to me and his beak snapped quickly as he said in Terran, 'Let's walk along the vats, human? You haven't seen the Ostraylean vats have you? They're somewhat larger than those in Brytan.'

'Why are you here?' I asked him. 'Have you been transferred? Had I known that I would have stayed on the mudflats and rotted – rather than see you again.'

He smiled. 'You're not being very flattering to yourself human. It's precisely because you're here that I came. To answer your query – I haven't been moved, I came at my own accord ostensibly to visit a Stringbrother, but in reality to foster something that will bring about the return of my former rank – and the destruction of the human race . . .'

We had climbed the ramps now and were on the high vat walls and I stopped and looked at him sharply.

'You mean the revolution?' I said.

'Correct. Your little revolt will prove to the Klees that humans are nasty little animals to be put down, once and for all. I've had my eyes on your absurd scheme from the start and I must say it's going rather well . . .'

I smiled now and said, 'You're doing this on your own – or with your Stringbrother. Certainly not with the sanction of any of the Klees. All I have to do is speak to someone in authority.'

'If you can get to see anyone in authority,' he mused, 'yes, perhaps – but then, you're not known here on this continent are you . . .?'

He was right. No one would listen to the ravings of an unknown human and take his word against a visitor from Brytan. I would be laughed at, even granting the fact that I found an audience willing to hear me.

'You're a very cunning creature Endrod.'

'I know. Infuriating isn't it? But it's the first time I've really had the chance to hit back since your father was executed – and this time I want the blow to be felt by all mankind.'

He paused, looking over into the sludge and I was tempted to push him – but Endrod was better with his wings than most, and would merely have glided to safety, thus scoring again.

'I would guess that your friend,' he said, turning to me again, 'is at this moment instructing a large native of the islands to gather recruits for the insurrection, when he comes with several hundred others to reinforce the large tower. I have already been approached by this male human with regards to an additional mating performance when I visited your nest of conspiracy some time ago – I have of course persuaded my military friends that we should grant this request.'

'Very magnanimous of you,' I retorted.

'Yes,' he agreed, still complacent. 'It is isn't it? But then I've always had a generous nature.'

'Why?'

'My peculiar human,' he stared up at me, 'who will soon be dust – you know why. Because that is when they will attack. I assume they will attempt to overpower some of the Soal aircraft crews at the mating and then head for one of the mushroom towers. Quite a neat little plan really. Anyway we'll soon see, won't we. I must remember to keep you locked up while the natives are repairing the tower – you might try to get word to your compatriot.'

I threw in a quick and hopeful question. 'Aren't you going to have me executed then?'

'Why yes, of course,' he replied, and my heart sank. He was playing his psychological games with me. 'Just as soon as we arrest the girl. You can watch her go first if you like – see, I am generous with you Cave.' This was the first time he had used my name to my face for as long as I could remember. He must have been enjoying himself immensely.

'You must understand me,' he continued. 'I am not interested in your death – all I ever asked for was revenge. Ultimately you will have to die, but first I must see you suffer and I must take delight in your humiliation – otherwise, where is the revenge? To kill you now would ruin everything I have dreamed of for many mouths. All you would be, is dead – and I would be left unsatisfied. Compare it to a sexual climax between humans – I must have my loveplay first to take the final thrust to a pitch of ecstasy.'

So it appeared Endrod had all the answers – and they were the right ones even though one of them at least had been arrived at by accident, for when Tangiia had asked for a reward in the form of an additional mating it was because the big Polynesian wanted to see Peloa again – not because it would provide a legal excuse for Stella's troops to muster on the shores of the enemy. Tangiia had not known about Stella's plans for him at the time Endrod had visited the island.

I was taken to my cell when Endrod finally tired of crowing over my fallen circumstances, and I stayed there for many days without seeing anyone except the guard. Endrod had heard about Reandeller and her mayflies and was delighted with the idea – that mayflies should remind me to live each day as if it were my last. He sent me the cage daily after obtaining a supply of nymphs from the seacraft, he said to remind me that at any time he could order my execution. The tactics were weak for he had already spoken out his heart and I knew that I would remain alive until Stella was eventually plucked from her dream of conquest. The peculiar thing was I hoped that it would be soon. I was reconciled to dying – after all, if the Soal drugs had not been available I would have died anyway, and lying on my sickbed I had had time to consider what the world had to offer. I loved two women, both of whom had been taken away from me. I hated being alone – and that was exactly my fate if I was allowed to live. To my mind death and loneliness cast the same shadows, with one difference – one is aware of one's loneliness. I preferred the oblivion of death to the experience of loneliness. A month in a sandstone cell nearly deranged my mind, and the bodies of the mayflies collected in the dust to mark the passing of the days – I kept them in a corner of the room. Endrod's psychological torture was far superior to Reandeller's original inspired game – for though his original reason for the mimicry had been invalidated by his promise to keep me alive, there was a second, more subtle, attack at my mental defences – he never sent more than a single mayfly at a time. Just one solitary insect, that flitted around the inside of the wire skull, probably wondering if all that time employed in reaching imago was worth the effort.

Once I tried crushing the cage, but another appeared the following morning as I guessed it would and that kind of retaliation only gave Endrod the satisfaction he craved – it showed that he was reaching inside me.

Endrod's determination to make me suffer mentally was not left at driving me insane with solitude. He came to my cell one morning just after I had finished eating. I had had a sparse breakfast of meat and wild corn, and was preparing for the weekly wash I gave myself in my drinking water – a habit that was hard to break since Stella had drummed into me the belief that dirt bred germs, and, despite what was good for the Soal, germs were harmful to humans if allowed to collect in large colonies about the skin or local environment.

I heard the sheet metal door slide back and Endrod appeared

just outside the entrance. He stayed there because the temperature in my cell was not thermostatically controlled and no Soal took chances of that kind. Though the short term danger was not as serious as they liked humans to believe, for I knew that those that had been caught in a quick temperature change could be revived in a thermochamber if they were taken to one within a reasonable time.

'I trust you are keeping well?' he mocked, employing the phrase my father often used to greet the Soal he served. I must have looked a pathetic sight with my long, matted hair and beard, stiff from dirt and sweat, and my skin filthy and covered in small sores. It was only by establishing a joint friendship with my guards that I managed to have my waste removed from the cell. Not that Endrod would have been concerned about a few faeces lying around the place – but Stella would have approved of my diligence.

'Have you taken her yet?' I asked as casually as I could. For all my silent hours of reconciling myself to my fate, I was still very much afraid.

'Not yet – give them time, the mating is not for several days. Your native friends have only just finished repairing our tower for us. I've come to take you for a walk – I'm sure you need one, it'll be good for your health.'

'Solicitous all of a sudden, aren't we?'

'Not both of us—just me. You care nothing for the state of my health,' he mocked.

I snarled. 'You're wrong there Soal – I care very much about the condition of your health – if only I had the means at my disposal to bring about the condition I would wish for you!'

'I'm sure you know what you mean, but I have no time for prattle – come with me.'

I hesitated and he turned and repeated the order. 'Come!'

This time I obeyed. We were accompanied by my guard, across the hardbaked ground to the edge of the accommodation area of the city, and into the mosaic of narrow streets that ran like multi-coloured rivers between tightly-packed spires and domes – all single or double storey here. The city was downwind for the prevailing breezes from the sludge tanks so that their odours blanketed the buildings. I filled my lungs several times which obviously amused Endrod but he said nothing.

I was eventually taken to a small eggshaped building and sat on a stool in a dark room. Endrod sent the guard outside and then began flicking some switches at the back of the room. I wondered what was going to come next. Endrod was not the type to take pity on me and my solitude and decide that I deserved some entertainment.

It was entertainment – of a sort. I was shown an aerial film of Tangiia's island. Some of the colours had had false brilliance added to distinguish the objects from the background scene.

'What are the red spots?' I asked.

Endrod readily answered me.

'Those are human people – and this broken blue patch here – that's the aircraft you stole from the mudflats. It has been covered in rocks to try to break up the shape – to camouflage it I believe the word is . . . Not a very good job you must admit.'

I stared at the screen. 'But there's at least a dozen or so red dots.'

Endrod smiled. 'Ah, well, they're getting confident as time goes by. And the female human – what's her name?'

'Stella . . .'

'Yes, Stella – she has to train those red dots into officers you see, and that's one thing that can't be done by proxy. They also have to be taught to use the aircraft – no doubt you trained the woman while escaping from the mudflats?'

I nodded.

'And now she's passing on her sparse knowledge to others – telling them how the disc drums will make wisps of gas out of Soal bodies.' His leathery palms were on my shoulders now and his rank breath hit me full in the face. In that instant I was tempted to smash both my fists into his foul skull and have done with it, but I knew that the moment I moved, even just a twitch, he would be three metres away. He might have been smaller than me but he was twice as fast moving.

'Well it won't be long before you're both together again and just so you don't forget how she looks . . .' he went back to the projector.

The camera angle moved and then zoomed in for a close up

of a human. It was Stella, full face, and I gasped. Her eyes were dark-ringed pits of light – the light of fanaticism – and her cheeks had hollowed to make her look witch-like and hard. She was waving her arms at someone and shouting – silently on the screen – and the order was driven home with a stabbing finger and what seemed a sharp reprimand. The picture faded.

'How did you take those?' I asked, my insides full of yearning for the girl.

'Does it matter? If you must know ... a pilotless craft about half a centimetre in length.'

'Can I go back to my cell now?' I had seen enough. Endrod observed that he had scored another victory by reaching inside me and crushing my heart with his coldblooded, psychological tactics.

'You can return to your room – but before you leave perhaps you would like to know that you have a visitor.'

I looked into his eyes to see if he was tormenting me further.

'No,' he said. 'You do have a visitor. An insignificant Soal that has been ordered out of his father's house in disgrace. His crime was trusting a human with a weapon – need I continue?'

Hope sprang to my breast.

'Lintar,' I breathed.

18

... blackness will rush in like the coming of a strong wind ...

Lintar

The early morning sun thrust itself through the slits in the high walls and spotlighted the old wooden beams above my head. Stare at something long enough and it becomes interesting. I fixed my eyes on those worn stalwarts of the roof and after a while began to see an artistry in the pitted texture of their surfaces. They became small, individual worlds which I compared, one against the other, to relieve the long days of boredom. The insects of Endrod no longer bothered me – they lived and died unnoticed by my eyes. It was now the wood that lay claim to my attention, and its inroads of scars and its various craters. There was a pastime in considering the manufacturers of those craters. Birds? Insects? Man? That led me to wondering who had made the building – it was of human, not Soal construction – and for what purpose. It reminded me of the humans that had built everything of box-like shapes on the volcanic island. Perhaps we had all, once upon a time, followed this religion I had discovered? My escape into the wood was interrupted by the sound of the door opening.

Some moments later the guard beckoned from the open doorway and I trudged, blinking, towards the light. She had come at last: the redness of the morning sun found colourful contemporaries in her hair as she stood, some ten metres away, between two Soal. Two? And I only warranted one guard? She must have given them a lot of trouble. Then I looked more keenly and recognized one of them – it was Lintar and he was talking rapidly to Stella, who appeared by her frown to be mildly irritated by what he was saying. Then they saw me and the conversation stopped. Stella looked surprised, whether at my appearance or because she had not been told that I was alive and well, I had no idea. But, on recovering, gave me a small tentative wave. I smiled back, encouragingly. She was people and I needed these. Not too many – just enough to talk to without becoming uninterested. There was a slight breeze blowing and it cooled my skin after the hot cell, causing me to shiver. My guard looked at me sharply and then, as if remembering I was a human and not a Soal, turned quickly away. Soal were not concerned with sensible temperatures, only actual, for their feathers were able to cope with the variations in sensible temperatures that light winds and small changes in humidity created.

Stella was then ordered to walk towards the accommodation area, probably to see Endrod, and she looked at me doubtfully. I nodded – we would be together soon enough. No sense in antagonizing them and risking a split. She did as she was told, walking with her head held high and defiant. Lintar came towards me.

'I expect you hate me?' I said, as he came near. He stopped and looked puzzled – then he realized what I was talking about.

'I did,' he replied, 'in the beginning, but I've grown used to being rebuffed by my father. He's grown to an age when he would be cantankerous anyway. How are you? Well?' Lintar seemed older himself, more mature.

'I have no diseases that I know of, but I'm not the hearty youth I was when you last saw me. Endrod's been keeping me boxed in there – it doesn't do my spirit any good. Weyym's been the recipient of a lot more begging orison lately.' I pointed to the cell.

Lintar replied: 'Perhaps I may be able to do something for you but I've lost a lot of my credibility lately: especially in this part of the world.'

I was sure the guard neither spoke nor understood Terran so I explained openly how Lintar might be able to regain a little of that trustworthiness. I told him about Endrod and his plans to allow a revolution among the humans to grow in order that he might use it as an excuse to begin a wholesale slaughter of mankind. '... so all you need to do is speak to someone in authority and reveal Endrod for what he is – a maniac who will risk Soal lives to satisfy his own personal hatred and ambition ...'

'Unfortunately you're too late,' said Lintar. 'It's happened, and the situation is not so clear-cut as you seem to believe. The Klees of Ostraylea and his Council have been involved in Endrod's plot from the beginning and approved of everything Endrod has done. Since they are the law here, even the deaths of several Soal will not alter Endrod's influence – in fact it increases his chances of getting other Klees to agree to the act of genocide. The deaths are so serious a matter that I think even my father will agree to Endrod's demands – though it will practically destroy him.'

'How many humans died?' I asked quickly.

He waved the question away, as if it was an insect buzzing round his eyes.

'You'll have to ask your female for the details Cave – I'm not in full possession of the whole story in any case.'

I nodded and could think of nothing else to say. Looking round I let my eyes feed on the scene around me. In front of me lay the Soal community with its beautiful streets and buildings, and the machine-tended lawns. On the edge of this, where the water bubbled through from the subterranean filters, the foliage had been allowed to grow wild and had almost reached jungle proportions. Some of the trees were taller than the spires that lanced the air before them and their heads tossed gently in a wind that had its origins in a cooler region than the one in which we stood.

Behind me was the tower, legs frozen in the act of striding across the desert and between and beneath those gigantic legs were the vat walks.

'Taking a last look?' asked Lintar. He had squatted on the ground now, and I joined him. The guard remained aloof, standing apart from us, but aware of our movements.

'I've taken many last looks. I seem to keep clinging to this ball in spite of Endrod ...'

'But this time he has you cold ... or perhaps not?'

I frowned. 'Meaning?'

Lintar began drawing designs in the dust. I looked for a message but after a while I realized he was just doodling. He said, 'Some of your ill-fated humans escaped after the skirmish and Endrod has no idea where they've gone. They entered one of those intercontinental tubes in three or four of the stolen aircraft. Endrod's people were not able to follow – as you know we need to acclimatize to each region in thermochambers. By the time charts of the tubes were produced the dissidents had disappeared. I have no doubt that Endrod wishes to know of their whereabouts urgently – and since the only one that can tell him . . .'

Stella! He did not need to say the name.

I said sharply. 'If he harms her . . .'

'He needs the information badly. You can see what sort of position it's going to put him in,' said Lintar. 'Incidentally, she too almost escaped the net. It took them two days to find her and strangely enough she was finally captured not far from here – just to the north. Don't you find that peculiar Cave?'

I did not answer but looked towards the building where Stella had been taken. I hoped she would talk because we were all finished anyway and I did not want her to suffer needlessly, in spite of the fact that it was she who had created this position.

'She'll be all right,' I said cheerfully. 'She's more than a match for Endrod. She's all nails and spit that woman – he'd better watch out for himself.'

'I'm inclined to agree with your assessment of the female but unfortunately she will not be allowed to get into a position where she can use her weapons.'

I declined to reply, but thought privately that Stella had more than tangible weapons. She was an Earthwoman, full of the cunning and guile that were inherent in her kind. Endrod had not come up against a person like Stella before and I was sure she would find some way of outwitting the Soal.

I turned to Lintar again.

'I won't miss you when I'm dead, because the Sennish tells us that death is a vacuum and I will have no more thoughts – but I want you to know that I have thought of you often since we parted and I still love you as I would love a brother.'

'Aren't you ashamed, to be so fond of a Soal – your enemy?' he smiled.

I remained serious in spite of Lintar's trying to wean me away from my mood – the talk made him uncomfortable.

'The Soal never have been my enemy. Circumstances, and a will stronger than my own, forced me into acts I wanted no part in. I have felt closer to the Soal than ever these past few months – though there are some humans of whom I have grown very fond. Tangiia – you would like him. He has the same impatience as yourself when things will not go right with life. And one or two women ...'

Lintar smiled again. '*One or two?* You are collecting them?'

I laughed now, aware that I was not going to pierce his armour.

'Probably the other way around my friend – they are collecting me. Each of them has a piece of me that she won't let go of. I'm afraid I'm only half a man in both their eyes – one of them thinks I'm too meek, and the other, too bold ... Weyym's eyes!'

'What's the matter?' asked Lintar. 'Why are you looking so pale?'

'I've just thought – one of them may be dead.'

'Then half of you is with her. I must say you only look half a man at the moment – but that's not your fault. I must go now. This is probably the last we shall ever see of each other ...'

'You've said that before.' I did not want an emotional scene. I was not likely to get one from Lintar but the way I felt at the moment any display of pity or unhappiness might evoke one from me.

I watched him walk away, carefully avoiding treading on the stones and thought how easy it was to love another creature – one not of your own kind. A lot easier than loving another human because there was no personal conflict involved. One was detached from another species and could watch and enjoy a rise status without feeling envious, competition being non-existent; unpleasant characteristics could be accepted as racial traits, whether they were individual or not; strange behaviour was rewarding, not suspicious; temporary rejection was a sign of independence, not of indifference. Lintar's casual acceptance of my impending execution would have been unforgivable in a human, but it was the Soal way of hiding grief. It made me feel wretched to watch Lintar lightly tripping across the ground which would soon receive my ashes but I could not censure him for it.

The guard was letting me have a little extra time, keeping a wary eye out for the approach of any superior – especially Endrod. I rose to my feet after a few moments more, ready to enter my solitude for a little while longer. As I did so I noticed Lintar's doodles in the dust. Strange marks. He had drawn a series of familiar-looking narrow inverted V's. They were like a cluster of tall boatless sails. Odd. I shrugged my shoulders. Another example of the separateness of our two races. Aesthetic communication was poor.

19

... In the beginning – nothing ...

Mission

Endrod had me moved to a longhouse on the shores of an artificial inland sea a few kilometres to the north. The sea was connected by an arrow-straight canal to the ocean and was salty, the water undergoing a long journey of filters before becoming the freshwater oasis springs to the south. This place, which no doubt Lintar had persuaded Endrod to move me to, had thermostats and the atmosphere was much more bearable than the sandstone cell. Here I waited for Stella.

When she finally came she looked badly bruised and shaken and after holding her tight for a few minutes I asked her if Endrod had her hurt badly.

'A little, but he believes he has time. Tomorrow he will try harder ...' her eyes glinted, 'but then tomorrow is plenty of time.'

Her attitude disturbed me.

'What's happening then?' I asked. Her answer was delivered in a triumphant tone.

'Wait and see – I can say one thing – Fridjt's coming. Anything else I say might cause you harm.' She put a hand to my cheek and stroked it while looking at me possessively.

'You mean Endrod might try to make *me* talk next – and I would probably crack.'

She nodded, giving me a sweet smile.

'But you'll know soon enough, my love. Tomorrow we may be breathing Soal-free air.'

I felt my eyes widen. 'It's not all over – the revolution?'

'It's just begun.'

I found it difficult to believe that the whole episode had not closed when Stella was captured, because she *was* the revolution – without her the others were lost. They had no leadership, no direction. I could not conceive of their doing anything without her. Especially Fridjt. He was a big man with a small brain – a dinosaur. Unless she had found someone else capable of assuming authority, and that was doubtful.

'Tell me about the fight,' I said. 'Did anyone I know get killed? Tangiia? Peloa . . .?' Then, as casually as I could, '. . . Tiptihani?'

There was no sign on Stella's face that she suspected Tiptihani of being my lover as she said, 'Peloa and Tiptihani? Of course, you met them briefly didn't you? No, they survived the skirmish – so did Tangiia. Actually Peloa didn't do very much – she's pregnant you know – but Tiptihani was a great organizer. Oh yes,' the light of remembrance came into Stella's eyes. 'She was with you when you were captured by the Soal, wasn't she? She told me she had to leave you and catch up with Tangiia – I felt like killing her for that, but when she said you had been poisoned by a stonefish I realized she had no choice. What happened? Obviously the Soal treated you.'

I recounted my experiences from the moment Tiptihani left me, leaving out the embellishments – the mayflies and my long hours of loneliness. The story was rather boring for the telling, and I began to feel that I had somehow let everybody down by not clawing and kicking at my escorts, making them drag me to my cell, refusing my food and attempting brilliant but foolhardly escape schemes. If I had told her a story like that however, Stella would not have believed me. She knew how I reacted to circumstances and she knew where I would make a stand and where I would bend.

When I had finished she nodded her head gravely. I think she understood some of the torment I had been going through in the cell. She then proceeded to tell her side of the story.

'I was very angry with you,' she began, 'for leaving the island without telling me first – but then you knew I would forbid you to go, that's why you didn't ask. After you left I passed the time familiarizing myself with the chiton, because once Tangiia was called for by the Soal and returned with recruits, you and I would need to train them in the use of the craft. So Fridjt and I together worked out all those details you had no time to pass on, by trial and error.

'When Tangiia returned we played everything in low key, making sure that the small island bore no marks of its large population of four, in order that the Soal who were to come for Tangiia did not get suspicious. They came at night however, and everything followed my plan quite smoothly – too smoothly in fact, and it was when Tangiia returned with the news that two thousand Polynesians had promised to join in the battle, resurrecting old war cries and dusty memories of ancestral bloodletting, that I began to get an inkling of our true position ...'

Had she known about Endrod's scheme at that time? If that was the case, Stella was so farsighted as to be almost a magician in the eyes of people like myself.

Stella continued. 'However, this setback was not as disastrous as it could have been – it would not necessarily interfere with the main plan. So I decided to go ahead – even though by now I was sure we were being watched. I calculated we would not be halted before we had actually done some physical harm to the Soal – otherwise we would have been stopped long before.

'You should have been with us Cave, it was magnificent. You've never been on a mating in these warm waters have you? I've never seen anything like it– thousands of canoes covering the waves for as far as you can see. Sail upon sail – and dyed all the colours of the spectrum ...'

Her eyes were alight as she recalled the images and I began to wonder if it had been the mating or the foray that had left the most impression on her. I did not remind her that I had not been on a mating of any kind ever.

'Excitement swept over the water as heavy and tangible as the scent of ambergris and it made me giddy and weak just to be near to the jostling craft – I was in Tangiia's canoe and luckily he managed to keep his head, and skirt the large area where all the boats were locked into a solid mass of heaving Satawals. We obviously lost a few of our people to the attractions of the main event, even one or two of our officers, but the majority remained loyal to the objective. To some men physical violence generates just as much excitement as sex. There was one man – an ugly little dwarf with blackened teeth, who took it on himself to be my personal bodyguard. Unfortunately he died in the attack, fighting a Soal just his height. I won't forget that midnight grin for a long time to come ...'

I listened, without interrupting, to her account of the attack – how they had surprised sixteen Soal craft on the beaches, had fought a running battle with the crews after gaining control of several of the vehicles and had finally managed to escape with six of the chitons. She and Tangiia had split from Fridjt and three others.

'Tangiia insisted on heading straight for his precious island, saying he had had enough,' continued Stella, 'and I had already sent Fridjt to the north via the Schooter tubes – which left me on my own ...'

'And what do you expect Fridjt to be able to do, with his craft? Hardly an armada Stella – not exactly the force with which to conquer the world.'

The evening was upon us now and I could hear the restless sounds of nocturnal creatures in the trees outside. I was having trouble focusing on Stella's face in the dim night lights inside the room and I needed to see her expression to put the real meaning to her words.

'Don't sneer Cave – Fridjt doesn't know it yet but he will save the world. He ...' But then she shut up, quickly, as if she had suddenly realized she was saying too much.

'What do you mean Stella?' I asked, gripping her shoulders, making her face me.

She pulled away, savagely. 'Leave me alone. You wouldn't approve because you don't yet understand.'

I barked in frustration. 'No, I never do understand, do I?'

I knew she would not say any more. I moved over to the doorway, which was of a transparent material. The guard stirred restlessly outside and I looked beyond him to one of the fibrous legs of the great tower, catapulting from the desert sand in a beautiful sweeping curve into the twilight's redness. The Soal had brought with them their own techniques in architectural structuring when they took the Earth by force, but though they also brought some new materials they found it necessary to use native metals for large constructions. Plaxsteel was the toughest of the Earth compound metals and they used it in conjunction with one of their stress-absorbing designs to form the intricate lattice-works of the towers that stroked the soft undersides of passing clouds.

It would take more power than the combined weapons that four chitons could muster to bring down a mushroom tower. I just could not see how it was going to be done and I felt that Stella was dreaming. I did not blame her. How could a girl from the mudflats know what physics were involved in bringing down a giant tower? To her, a Soal weapon could destroy any solid, whether it was a floating log or the metres-thick metal spar of a tower. She had turned the former to gas with the chiton guns – she expected the latter to follow suit given the same treatment.

'You've lost your war Stella,' I said over my shoulder, and was surprised at the despair in my own voice. 'You're a clever girl and I don't know how you managed to get this far but it's over now. There's nothing Fridjt can do, and it would be a kindness if you could stop him trying.'

In complete contrast to my tone, hers was buoyant and full of optimism.

'It seems silly to keep repeating it but *we haven't lost yet*! If only I could tell you – but I don't trust you fully. You've got too many principles, and they're the wrong ones as far as my mission is concerned. If I told you what this was all about – really all about – you'd rush off to your precious Lintar and tell him everything. It's much bigger than you think, Cave – you'll be surprised how big.'

I turned and faced her again. Her dirty red hair fell over her face – one black eye stared sorrowfully between its curtains: blackened by Endrod no doubt. She would withstand his torture until doomsday if she thought it was important to him that she cracked – he was one of those that had helped to destroy her children.

'The others – the Polynesians – they went home?'

She nodded.

'Endrod felt that they would die soon enough anyway. Why clutter up his accommodation areas with scruffy vermin when a few puffs of gas will soon clear them out of their retreats?

When he gets his licence he'll have his fun. Did you know he's now in line for the position of Klees of Filipine? At the moment he's an honorary Military Head. Ambitious little bastard!' I moved away from her again. My desire for information was just leading us into petty quarrels. Outside, an unseen hand was skimming the building with bladed bats. I tried to catch their details as they curved in and away but the light was bad, and the bats too fast.

In the room the air was still. So still that I could hear a large moth fluttering its dusty wings against one of the night lights. Did the moth consider that it too was in prison? Or was the room large enough for the creature to believe it was free? What size does a prison have to be before a man is aware of his confinement? Someone confined to one room – one building – definitely considers himself a prisoner. What about a defined area, an island or a country? It would depend on the length and breadth of the person's mind, the extent or limitation of previous movement. Someone confined to a room for a long period and then allowed to roam at will over an enclosed country might feel he had freedom. How about a world then? We were all prisoners of the Earth – its atmospheres and temperatures were our walls – did we consider ourselves prisoners? The answer for myself was, yes. I wanted to escape to other worlds, be they the size of a small room or almost sun-size. For Tangiia, freedom was to be able to roam his ocean – if he could not visit the neighbouring ocean it would not have worried him. Peloa would be happy with an atoll. The dead old lady on volcano island, happy with her house. It was an attitude of mind.

Poor Weyym, I thought suddenly. Weyym was a god, with a mind that expanded like gas to fill the space available. Even if the universe was infinite, he was crouched inside it, straining at its walls like a mouse in cupped hands. Always, all ways, a prisoner.

'Peloa and her mother – I suppose they're still with Tangiia?' I asked.

'I suppose so.'

'And Fridjt? Where is he and his men?'

Her face darkened.

'Somewhere to the north,' she said tight-lipped.

'Where? The Soal will have them wherever they are.'

'There are still some places which the Soal do not visit – the arctic circle for one . . .'

'Then why didn't we go and live there Stella?' I blurted. 'Instead of starting this foolhardy war. Maybe it's not too late . . .'

'It is too late,' she snapped. 'Much too late.'

The night was black as Stella's face, and I sat and listened to the waves breaking with regular monotony on the sand. A slight onshore breeze was blowing and ruffling the feathers of the Soal outside.

Both of us were watching for the first sign of Fridjt but as the evening grew longer Stella became more and more nervous, screwing her fingers together and biting at her bottom lip. I took one of her hands thinking to comfort her, but her anxiousness was such that she jerked it from my grasp.

Then I heard her whisper. 'Come on you stupid man, where are you?'

'Who?' I asked in an equally low voice.

'That idiot Fridjt,' she replied. 'I had to make him the key to the whole operation. In the beginning I wanted you for this part but,' she turned her eyes on me, her red hair catching some of the light from the rods in its folds, 'when it came to choosing I just couldn't sacrifice you. I know that when the time came you weren't there anyway but I had already made the choice when we first landed on the island. I loved you enough to let you live, even though Fridjt might ruin the operation where you would have succeeded. I am not seeking your approval now. I just wanted you to know that I value you above my mission and the lives of all humans be they Martians or Terrans.'

20

... In the end – nothing ...

Hit

'What do you mean by that?' I barked at her. Something was bad, I could sense it. Stella had done something, I knew, for which I at least would be sorry. The Soal at the door turned to glance at us, casually, but then resumed his previous stance, looking out to sea.

'Cave,' she replied, 'I'm going to be honest with you for once. About the only completely true words I have told you before this are that I love you. That I swear. Most of the rest has been lies. I'm a Martian ...'

I felt a tingling go through my skin as she said it but at the same time I wanted to laugh.

'There are no Martians,' I said. 'Martians are fictitious fun-figures that only appear in Soal jokes.'

'I am,' she repeated firmly. 'I'm a human whose forebears left Earth to colonize Mars and whose ancestors fought the Soal from subsurface colonies and, unlike our Terran cousins, man-aged to beat them. I know this sounds like a campfire story to you Cave, but I was born on Mars, trained for a mission to Earth and am, so far as I know, the only Martian agent ever to survive the Soal barrier. Those "lightning" storms you love so much are not natural at all – they are the primary function of the mushroom towers in action. The towers form a network of beams that destroy anything that they come into contact with.'

'Then how did you get through?' I questioned suspiciously.

'I made it because I was lucky – no other reason. Many agents have died trying to get through. In the beginning it was whole flotillas of ships. We put our greatest brains to work on recovering the Earth. Some say we should have used our resources and intelligence in making Mars a fitter place to live – but in keeping the environment harsh we kept our minds and bodies tuned to the task in hand. Had we made ourselves comfortable we might have given up the struggle and accepted the Soal dominance over our mother world as inevitable.

'The ship I came in was ingenious in design and took many Earth months to construct it. It consisted of many canisters that slotted into one another – basically the idea was that while the outer shell was disintegrating under the Soal beams, which took time, if only a millisecond, the next hull, still travelling, would be that much further inside the web of beams – and so on. It was calculated that the innermost canister would be inside the network as the penultimate shell disintegrated.'

'And you were within the innermost canister?'

'I and three others. Two of us landed on the mud between Brytan and Hess. My companion's soft-landing gear failed. He died on impact. The other two I never saw or heard of again. They may even still be alive for all I know.'

I shifted uncomfortably under her intense gaze. It was not that I did not *want* to believe her now, but the whole thing was incredible – not the least that it had taken the Martians very many months to penetrate the Soal barrier and then with only one person. Nevertheless I had always considered Stella strange, in that she had too much knowledge for one whose life had been spent without any form of learning except a mother's words.

'How can I know you are telling the truth now?' I asked.

'If Fridjt comes, then you will know,' she said. Again, that cold stare that frightened me so much. What was going to happen? Something terrible. But I dared not ask her for fear of the answer.

'But the baby and the rest?' I finished weakly.

'The baby was real enough,' she said, surprisingly with some bitterness in her voice, 'but it wasn't Fridjt's. It was some Weyym-high bastard that raped me in a needle tower one night. Fridjt was in the segment above and he heard and beat the man's brains against a stone. It was not the first rape but it was an unlucky one. It got me pregnant. Here,' she offered a lobe of her ear and an invitation. I fingered it gingerly.

'Have you ever felt that before? When we were mating?'

'Our couplings were always too quick to feel *anything*,' I replied testily. 'What is it? It feels like a stone.'

She laughed. 'It's a Soal detector. It tells me when one or more of their craft is near by, by gentle vibration. It's doing it now. That's probably a patrol. How else do you think I . . .'

Suddenly there was an enormous explosion. We were both thrown to the floor and the whole sky seemed to be alight with sparks and splinters of flame. The Soal in the doorway was gone, his light frame lifted and thrown into the night like a rag.

Then came another, and yet another explosion, each more deafening than the last. I screamed, clutching my head as the concussion burst one of my eardrums causing me intense pain. My eyes, screwed tight, were blinded by the light and I could feel the ground moving beneath me. A second later the building collapsed around us but fortunately the wall we were leaning against still stood, with the taller roof supporting it.

Next came the screeching of metal grating against metal, that penetrated the ringing in my good ear, and I knew the tower was falling. We were finished if it came our way because its size would ensure that everything for a kilometre along the shoreline would be destroyed in a tangle of giant metal girders. Even falling in the opposite direction it would hit the ground hard enough for the springboard effect to flip us into the air, as objects will jump on a table when somebody bangs a fist down hard on its surface. I heard Stella crying, but not for help. She was screaming into my ear.

'We've done it. The tower . . .'

A fourth blast, of equally terrifying proportions, drowned her words and I opened my eyes to see a star nova just a kilometre above our heads.

The tower did not fall. When the dawn came and the acrid smoke began to clear, we looked upwards to see a crease on one of its five corners. The section above the buckle was leaning over as if it were bowing stiffly from the waist. It looked like a giant stick insect bending down to inspect the lower orders of life, its mushroom head leaning rakishly on its spindly neck.

The spot that was warped was black from the impact of the missiles that had struck it – chitons hurtling into the girders at three thousand kilometres an hour. For Stella, if that was her real name, had told me after the thunder and flashing had ceased, and all we could hear was a wind rushing in from somewhere above the world, that it was Fridjt and Lipsua who had bent the tower – with their bodies. While I had slept in my small cell last night, Stella had been to the Schooter tubes that approached the Ostraylean coast, and in the wheelhouses had turned the last four in an arc which curved towards the tower. Unwittingly Fridjt had sacrificed himself, and those other poor humans he had recruited, in order to gain Stella the entry onto Earth which she desired for her Martians.

'You murdered him,' I accused her, but without remonstration.

Black spaceships with spiky prows were descending now and from the bellies of these craft came smaller, arrowhead shapes. Wings glinted with the brightness of weapons, and winked white spots as they attacked the ground below them.

'Don't feel like that Cave,' she begged. 'It was the only way I could do it – the only way I could see. I didn't want him to die. I *liked* Fridjt. He was a real man.'

I did not know what to say. She felt she was right in sacrificing Fridjt in order to regain the Earth for the humans. Could I tell her she was wrong and condemn her for something I did not understand? I had no idea what her indoctrination had been. Perhaps she was not even responsible for her actions. It was possible that her mind was not hers to control but manipulated by one of her Martian superiors. Certainly her actions were motivated by an intense hatred for the aliens that had conquered Earth, and by an unshakable sense of duty to those she considered in authority.

I would never understand her – she was more alien to me than any Soal I had ever met. Not for the first time I wished I were something else – a Soal, another alien, anything but a human.

'*Why* did you do it Stella? What made you come to Earth – you could not have had any idea what life was like here. Why didn't you Martians settle for Mars and leave the Earth to the Soal? If your tenacity had been absent we might all have lived a peaceful life down here. No wonder they gave us a hard time with you banging on the front door of the sky all the time, yelling to get in. Earth had been lost to your ancestors, not to you . . .'

Stella gave me one of her characteristic hard looks.

'Earth is human by right – we were spawned from the very soil on which you stand. We didn't grow from Martian clay – the seed of life sprang up here, amongst these minerals. They pull us back, like a magnet, to where we belong. We are as much an ingredient of Earth as kaolin is of granite – without the kaolin there is no granite. Granite is a hard rock, able to resist pressures and blows – but wash away the clay, and the feldspar and mica fall apart, leaving nothing.'

'Well something pulls you back anyway,' I said, 'because you came, and we can't change that. I just hope that those minute pieces of Fridjt and Lipsua that rained on us last night don't hate you too much for having taken their lives. The Universal Weyym knows . . .'

'Weyym is a Soal god,' she snapped, 'and this part of the universe at least has no use for that kind of god. Our god walks on two legs and carries a gun in his hand.'

'Guns have never solved problems,' I argued. 'They only create them.'

She replied, logically. 'They solved them for the Soal. Those birdmen you love so much laid waste to this planet of ours with little compunction – if any. Admittedly millions managed to escape to Mars and the moons of Jupiter but many died through lack of resources – our colonies there were not equipped to deal with such a flood of refugees. From the few people now left here on Earth, a miserable handful, the Soal must have systematically executed the survivors until only the grovellers remained.'

'That is a lie Stella,' I said emphatically. 'They just prevented us breeding for a few years, separating the males and females. It doesn't take long to deplete a race in that manner.' I paused. The woman exasperated me beyond endurance.

'Look, how would you react if your world – Mars, or Earth – was dying slowly? You'd go out and look for another place to live wouldn't you? First you'd look around for suitable places within reach – the Soal ships are equipped with interstellar drives but their ability to sustain the speeds required is limited. The sort of worlds you would look for would be like the one described in your folklore – a planet covered in vegetation and wildlife . . . a planet where it was possible to live on the surface. The Soal had such a planet aeons ago but their sun began pulling in its bodies towards it and the surface became too hot even for the thermostats the Soal developed to deal with their predicament. Finally they went below the surface and began preparations to evacuate their world. They built starships. But by that time they had lived in a constant temperature for so long their bodies needed it . . .'

Stella was not listening, she was staring towards the sky.

'Wait till you see a real man Cave – then you'll know why I call them gods . . .'

21

... My form is infinite ...

Gods

The new gods were tall arrogant men and women, with narrow features and high foreheads. They were Stella's people. They had the same assurance and easy confidence. They strode, not stepped. They commanded, not requested.

We lay in the ruins of the Soal building for the rest of the night, afraid to move in case either a Soal mistook us for one of the enemy, or a blast-happy Martian cut us down.

When the sun arose we knew that those Soal, the ones who had not found their way to spaceships or the thermostatically controlled chambers into which they retreated when they accidentally experienced a temperature drop, would die with their nerve-ends aflame with pain.

We stood together, as the dawn came over Oceania, and regarded the devastation around us. A tall man approached us with a weapon clamped to his forearm.

'You two – out of there. Quickly.'

We did as we were told, Stella slightly more defiantly than myself.

The man was covered in an artificial skin and there were blue discs on his breast. His head was encased in a protective hemisphere of metal. A sneer crossed his face, for what reason I could not imagine.

'Naked! You must be Dirt-loafs.'

'Dirt-loafs?' I repeated, bewildered.

He was looking Stella up and down, still with the same sneer.

'Wipe your face clean Captain,' snapped Stella, 'my name is

Stella Masteen. *Major* Masteen. I'm the Martian agent that got you slow spinners onto the dirt.'

The sneer faltered and the owner lost a tiny drop of his self-importance.

'You're too small,' he tried, attempting to regain his former air of superiority.

'Call me by my rank when you address me,' said Stella coldly. 'You know very well I was chosen for this mission because of my small stature. By your accent you're a Westerner and therefore probably in the Newameric battalion. If you doubt my word *now* Captain, you can rest assured that when I receive the rewards I shall surely get for my part in this – and I shall be entitled to the honours of a world heroine – I shall bust you down as far as I can get you.'

The Martian hesitated no longer. He snapped his body rigidly upright – a posture that must have been as painful to maintain as it was to watch – and told the 'Major' that he apologized for not having recognized her and that she would no doubt realize that he was exhausted through much travel and fighting, and then he babbled on about our being dirty and in a similar condition to other 'dirt-loafs' they had picked up during the night.

'Why does he keep saying that?' I whispered to Stella, as we accompanied the captain to a near-by airplane.

'What? Dirt-loaf? They call Earth people that on Mars because while the Martians have been labouring for centuries to free Earth from the Soal, the humans down here have been loafing their time away doing nothing – or seemingly doing nothing.'

'But they – the Martians . . .' I still could not think of Stella as a Martian, 'they could not know the situation on Earth. Why did they just assume we were doing nothing?'

Stella looked at me coldly.

'Well, they guessed it. The people that still lived on Earth at the time it was attacked were those unimaginative people who lacked the courage to emigrate to Mars. They were soft, dull men and women that liked the comfortable mundane existence that their secure little world offered them. We guessed that they would capitulate to the Soal without a murmur, and that their insipid descendants would follow their lead and kowtow to the birdmen. And we guessed right.'

'But we did eventually revolt . . .'

'Only because I, a Martian, came amongst you and pumped a bit of strength into your weak . . .' She paused and studied my face. 'Look,' she continued, 'I don't want to fight with you Cave. I love you.' She touched my face, but I jerked away angrily, just in time to see the sneer returning to the Captain's features as he regarded this interplay.

We were taken to a derelict Soal building which the Martians had made their headquarters for this area. On the way we saw many Soal bodies, some twisted and bearing the scars of heat beams or explosive missiles : some unmarked but curled in a ball, the telltale death posture of a Soal caught in a swift temperature change. Here and there a torn wing fluttered in the breeze like the sad battle flag of a defeated army. What agonies those poor creatures must have gone through ! I felt no elation : no triumph.

We also saw many more Martians who strode by us with flickering glances at our dirty naked forms but without losing their disdainful air. It gave me an inferiority complex just to see their tall straight bodies, muscles forming gentle contours on the sheer, tight artificial skins which covered them from neck to ankles. Even their feet were encased in some sort of thick material which added to their height. They moved much more slowly and with less bounce than Earthmen did though. There was a certain heaviness in their tread and I was glad that we had something over them – even if it was only agility.

We were taken inside the building where a Martian with two red discs on his breast was discussing something with three of his men. He looked worried and was saying, '. . . it's bound to happen at first. We're lucky down here – in the northern hemisphere everything's gone wild.' He turned just after we entered and the Captain that had escorted us was chanting a monologue which told how he had found us and that the female claimed to be a Martian agent. He never reached the end of his report because Stella shouted delightedly across the room.

'Alan ! Colonel Alan Riderman !'

Red discs peered at her more closely and a smile suddenly broke out across his craggy face. He ran a hand through his silvery hair.

'Damn me – Stella Masteen! We'd given you up for dead. Where's John Staines and the others? Were you responsible for opening the door?'

Stella crossed the room and gave the gentleman a hug, which embarrassed everyone in the room including the recipient of the affection.

'In answer to your question – yes, I was the one who let you in – Cave and I. He's a Terran ...'

'Dirt-loaf,' I interrupted. 'Let's get our terms correct Stella.'

The Colonel stared at me with a puzzled expression on his face and our escort shifted uncomfortably from one foot to the other. It was good to see that the armour of superiority could be pierced.

Stella continued after a short pause.

'I believe the others are dead, Colonel. They had some bad luck on entry. John definitely – the others *almost* certainly.'

He looked at her with an incredulous expression on his face.

'Then you did all this alone?'

She had just begun nodding happily, anticipating the water-falls of praise that were about to begin to drop from the lips of her peers, when I interrupted again.

'Not *quite* alone,' I said, 'there are one or two dead bodies out there on an island that had something to do with it, when they were alive. There are also,' I added, looking at her pointedly, 'one or two other men and women whose bodies will never be found. Perhaps a smear or two on the mushroom tower will testify to their unwitting sacrifices. Apart from that,' I turned my attention back to Riderman, 'yes, I suppose Stella did it alone.'

Stella glared hard at me and then said brightly to the Colonel, 'Take no notice of Cave. He's upset because we lost one or two men in the revolt. He's not used to violence – or being a hero. You can imagine what these Terrans have gone through. Did you know the Soal would not allow them to meet each other? Each Terran from the age of fourteen Earth years was ordered into solitary confinement for the rest of his life. Apart from the allowed mating periods every three Earth years they never saw another human being.'

'We had some information of the sort,' replied a dark-haired, handsome Martian with a deferential nod towards the Colonel, 'isn't that right sir? We learned about the degrading, disgusting practice of "matings" when interrogating the Soal. They seemed to consider they were right to let that sort of thing go on.' He finished his sentence with a snigger. I was beginning to understand why Stella had been so instantly demanding in her lovemaking – so inexperienced in the art of foreplay. These people were prudes. Sex was a subject for closed doors.

'The Soal you "interrogated",' I said coldly, 'did not conquer the Earth, nor did they make the laws. They were born into the society we had here and they accepted that their forefathers had reasons for making such rules. They were not completely to blame for the condition in which you found the Earth.'

'So they were all good little aliens?' the man with the black hair snorted. 'Misunderstood, but pure in heart.'

'No,' I replied calmly. 'Some were good, some were bad. Not very different from us really. What you must realize is that many of them had never seen a human being. To the ordinary Soal we were strange animals living on the small islands of the world. Only the military had any physical contact with us and they tended to be dispassionate soldierly types – not always unsympathetic to our hard life style, but tending to consider circumstances in the light of rules to be adhered to, rather than what was moral. It was the classic situation where on one hand those that made the laws were divorced from the results of those laws and therefore unwittingly blind to their effects, and on the other, those that saw that the laws were carried out had no power to change them.

'The power is at the top of the line, with the brains. The muscle at the bottom, with the unintelligent. Unfortunately, contact with the results of bad laws comes at the wrong end of the line.'

The Colonel said to Stella, 'You've picked up a bit of a scholar here.'

Stella told them about my being raised amongst the Soal and

added that my sympathies were not always constant in their direction.

Riderman then addressed me.

'Anyway, fella, I'm afraid I'm near the bottom of the line, an unintelligent soldier, and I have to consider my orders, which are to prepare this world for the coming of some five hundred million people and at the moment we have grave problems with weather in the north – and certain parts of the south. Terrible storms have broken out all over the world, and there's flooding and Mars knows what. It's almost as if the weather's been harnessed for so long it feels it has a right to go wild for a while. We're not used to weather either, living in our sub-surface cities, so we're attempting to repair and reactivate the Soal thermostatic system . . .'

'Five hundred million people?' I gasped. Surely there was not that much life in the whole universe.

'Yes,' answered the Colonel. 'It's only a start we're looking for now but later on we should be able to allow a few more millions in to relieve the overcrowding on Mars. Then we can start on Mercury and the various moons; Ganymede for example.' He rambled on while my mind drowned in a picture of millions of bodies, covering the Earth like a ball of maggots.

22

... my energy boundless ..

Chambers

'This place stinks!' remarked our escort as he led the way to where the Soal thermostatic chambers stood. The chambers, containing those Soal that had managed to reach them before the temperature rose from 20 to 26·7 degrees, had been collected from all over Ostraylea and placed by the shore for transportation to Yusat, the Martian headquarters in the northern hemisphere.

I had given up arguing with that remark. It was pointless. The Martians had their idea of what was an acceptable atmosphere, and I had mine.

I was wearing one of the artificial skins – it was made of soft, blue-coloured material and had the facility of keeping me cool when the day was hot, and warm when the weather was cold. I had to admit I liked it. The Martians called it a quilter.

Stella was with me but she had been distant since the Martians had arrived. This was possibly because I could not stop criticizing everything the newcomers did or said. She had taken to frequenting their bawdy houses late at night and I knew for certain that she had mated with one of the Martian officers – the dark-haired handsome giant that had been in the Colonel's regional headquarters. I had refused to shave my beard, but I had washed in soap-water, a detergent that helped to remove dirt, and I had promised her that I would not finger my nose, or spit inside buildings – neither of which I had done much of anyway.

'How much farther?' I asked the sergeant.

'Two tunnels maybe – maybe less.'

'What the Weyym is two tunnels?' I asked Stella truculently.

'About a kilometre,' she answered.

Her voice was sullen and I made a mental note not to upset her further. It was I who had asked to walk anyway. I wanted to see the tree tops glistening with the recent rain and watch the sunlight running like a basilisk over the blue folds of water. In a poetic mood, and sick of the inside of buildings, I wanted to cleanse my soul with nature.

The Martians had not repaired the mushroom tower but they had got to work on the buildings, bridges and communications. Storms were their main problem and in Ostraylea we had experienced some fierce winds carrying dust and sand, that gave the building robots problems with their joints.

Eventually we reached the thermostatic chambers: low rectangular metal structures on floater bars. We entered the first by means of the locks and after a short time came to the centre of the chamber, where, in the dimly lit interior, I perceived about two dozen Soal huddled together pathetically in groups of five or six. They were in *stool*.

'Twenty-one in here,' said the sergeant, his voice echoing through the metal room. 'Recognize any?'

I took a hard look at each one in turn but it was difficult.

'Can't see their faces properly, when they're in *stool*,' I remarked, 'and the light is bad.'

One of the Soal shuffled his feet but still kept his head buried deep between his shoulders. I knew that this was not their thinking stance and that they were aware of us. It was the *stool* they went into when they were deeply ashamed.

'Perhaps the sergeant can shake one of them into attentiveness?' suggested Stella, not without a malicious bite to her voice. 'I believe they kick ostriches up the backside when they bury their stupid heads in the sand.'

'I don't recognize any of them,' I said, and left the inner chamber. After a while the other two followed me and we visited several more chambers. I gave the same reply to the sergeant's question in each one as we entered. Finally we came to a chamber, much the same as the others, where the sergeant intoned, 'Eighteen in this one.'

I could see at once he was wrong. There were two groups of six and one of four.

'Sixteen,' I corrected him.

His eyes narrowed and swept the chamber, taking in all the corners.

'Should be eighteen,' he emphasized. 'There's two missing.' His hand reached for his weapon and snapped it clear of its thigh clip.

Stella said, 'Look! In the wall!'

We followed her finger and our eyes rested on two dark rectangular cavities. We crossed to them and I gingerly felt around inside.

'Nothing there,' I told them, 'and there's a back to it, so it's not an escape hatch.'

'They don't need an escape hatch,' remarked the sergeant frowning, 'we saw no need to lock them in. They can't go outside – the temperatures vary too much, night and day. Especially now, while the weather's pissing about. Must have had suits of some kind in those little closets. I think they've bunked on us.'

Stella looked grim.

'We'll have to wake one of them now – to get some answers.'

I nodded reluctantly and the sergeant lifted the nearest Soal and began to shake him.

'Not that one,' I said. 'He probably doesn't speak Terran. That one over there.' I indicated a Soal with military wing-markings.

The first Soal was dropped and the second lifted roughly. After several shakings his head emerged and he regarded us with miserable-looking eyes.

'Where are the two Soal that are missing?' I asked.

'Gone,' he answered directly. 'We ... we don't know where.' The sergeant shook him hard.

'Don't do that!' I said sharply. 'It's not necessary.'

Then to the Soal.

'Were they wearing suits of some kind?'

'Yes,' the Soal replied. 'Only those of their rank are permitted to wear them. We are to stay here and die, for the ships have a limited capacity.'

'Why are you telling us this?' inquired Stella. 'Are you bitter at being left behind?'

The Soal gave a crossed-beak smile.

'Not bitter. That would be stupid. We have our laws about who should, and should not go, and we accept them. Perhaps they go to an uglier death? Who can tell? I merely give you this information because it will only serve to enrage you. Humans anger easily and nothing grieves them more than being fooled. You will never find the ships, for they are too well hidden. You *may* find the two Soal, because one of them is so incensed with the desire for revenge on some human called Cave, he has thrown away all caution.'

Dread pulled at my stomach muscles.

'What was this Soal's name?' I asked.

'He was a Military Head. A new one called Endrod. You have heard of him?' The smile mocked me as he recognized fear in my face.

'I pity this human called Cave, for Endrod will not rest until he has torn open the man's throat. I have never seen such intense hatred in any . . .'

'Enough!' I said trembling. 'I can deal with Endrod. Put that miserable creature down sergeant, and I suggest you check the other chambers to see if any more of your prisoners are missing.'

I strode from the chamber and out into the sunlight, hardly caring if the locks closed behind me or not. Outside, in the brightness of the day, my fear began to dissipate. After all, Endrod could only survive for so long – the suits must have a limited life – and anyway the fleet, wherever it was, would not wait for him forever. He would surely not place revenge above his own chance of escaping from Earth.

A moment later, Stella was by my side. Desire for violence had once again possessed her small demonic frame.

'Now's our chance to get that little bastard Endrod for all the wrongs he has done you, Cave. We'll have to draw him out, using you as bait.'

I was horrified.

'You don't know Endrod, Stella. He always carries out his threats. He'll kill me before you can stop him.'

'Don't be such a coward Cave. You do this for me and I'll . . .'

'And you'll do what Stella? Give up your new boyfriend?

Stop opening your thighs for the troops? What?' I interrupted coldly.

She stared at me hard. We were back on the old battleground again, just Stella and I, claws out and fangs drawn.

'You'll do as you're told you bastard,' she said evenly. 'The Colonel will make sure of that. Then, when we've got Endrod we'll get him or his companion to lead us to the ships.'

I shrugged my shoulders helplessly. What could I do? The Colonel's loins were not so old, they would not appreciate the intimacy of Stella's willing bed. She had me every way I turned.

'Weyym will send you a gift one day,' I said finally. 'With any luck it will get you right between the shoulder-blades.'

'That'll make a change,' she replied coolly, 'from getting it between the thighs, won't it?'

I refrained from answer.

23

... my life, a spark ...

Stars

'Why is it so important to catch him?' I asked Riderman. My
visitors had joined me on the balcony of my accommodation.

The evening was cool and we were sitting in manufactured
seats called chairs, an alcoholic drink at our elbows. We were
studying the wigs of the palms and watching the fruit bats
float gracefully from tree to tree. On the water, purple bars of
light rippled like ribbons in the wind.

Stella answered for him. She was at our feet, girlishly dang-
ling her legs over the edge of the balcony. Her hair was now cut
short and in the shape of doves wings, and on her face above
the left cheek, she wore two stars that flashed red and white
alternately.

'Because we must find the Soal fleet,' she said. 'The Soal have
interstellar drives in their space ships. Once out of the atmosphere our ships would be unable to catch them.'

'We have units out searching for them of course, but they are
masters at camouflage, the Soal.'

The Colonel sipped his drink moodily after this remark, making the ice cubes clink against the side of the metal goblet.

For the past few nights and days I had been propped up on
the balcony waiting for Endrod to come and kill me. I had almost died twice – once when a wild dog slunk by in the early
dawn, and once when a fruit bat skimmed the corner of the
house. I thought grimly how Tangiia would have dealt with the
bats and birds, and wished he were here to deal with Endrod.
Tangiia was not a violent man by nature but he was big and
able, and he hated Soal.

I had chosen my quilter to go with the colour of the wall behind me, so as to make a poor target. It also annoyed me to notice that Riderman edged his chair away from mine if I leaned too close to him.

'Be careful you aren't hurt,' I grumbled.

'What do you mean?'

'I mean, make sure you aren't too close to me when Endrod comes to kill me.'

This was designed to anger him, and it was succeeding – then something unforeseen intervened. He placed a hand on my arm.

'I ...' began Riderman, wagging a slim finger. But then the finger curled slowly upwards and my eyes went to his face. The agony in his expression made me start backwards in terror. His own eyes went up into his skull, the narrow lips twisted into oxbows and the fingers of his right hand sank into my arm like steel talons.

The most horrible part of this scene was the fact that no sound had been made and Stella was unaware that anything was happening. She was still staring out into the trees, humming softly to herself. Then the pain hit me as blood began seeping through my quilter. I screamed, long and loud: Riderman's nails had reached bone.

'Get him off me,' I shrieked, trying to prise out the fingers. As Stella turned, the Colonel stood on his feet, and with one lunge at the metal balcony rail deliberately cracked his head open. The force of the blow killed him instantly and immediately the fingers relaxed, I jumped the rail, falling heavily into the bushes below. I had no desire to suffer the same fate as Riderman. I did not blame him for smashing his own skull – any man on the receiving end of a Soal brainstinger would have done the same. The demons tearing away at a man's mind, conjured up by the weapon, are so horrific they do not even allow the pitch of his scream to come down to an audible sound. The only way out is to destroy the mind, which is what Riderman did.

I scrambled through the bushes, my injured arm hurting so badly. I glanced back only once, to see an expression on Stella's sharp features which may have been concern for my welfare, or the outward signs that she too was on the receiving end of a brainstinger. It did not stop me. I intended to get well away from that weapon.

I ran, perhaps twenty metres, crashing through the undergrowth, before pausing for a breath. As I stopped, wondering which way was the opposite direction from my adversary, I saw a slight movement in the bushes only a few metres away.

He had me! Endrod had me. There was no decision to make. With panic in my breast I ran straight for the spot and flung myself on top of a grey form. It struggled beneath my weight but I held it until the wriggling ceased. Then I wrenched the head round to stare through the face-plate: the chill of fear went through me once again.

It was not Endrod.

The Soal eyes stared out at me with a fear of their own.

'Where is he?' I whispered harshly. 'Where's Endrod?'

The eyes went over my shoulder and I turned just in time to see a shape soaring down from the branches of a high tree. A second later it was on my back and claws impatiently searched my face for my eyes.

'Endrod!' I screeched. I put my hands over my head, grabbing loose material from the thermosuit and flung the Soal overhead. He landed, not heavily, in a shrub, was on his feet in a second, and scrambling back towards me. It was Endrod. His eyes, narrow with hatred and urgent with desire to kill me, transfixed me for a moment. The 'stinger was in his hand and he levelled it with my head.

I flung myself sideways, at the same time grabbing a dead branch. The little Soal followed my movements, sweeping with the brainstinger. On my knees, I threw the wood, in desperation, like a spear.

It struck his face-plate, knocking him backwards off his feet. Jumping forward, I clutched at his legs and, holding his ankles, swung him bodily at a tree. The bones in his light frame splintered on impact, one of them coming through the thermosuit, and after two more swings I dropped him, partly in revulsion and partly in sheer exhaustion. Panting, I watched his body twitch once more, then it lay still on the ground.

As I began to regain my breath I turned to look at Endrod's companion. He shook his head and waved a hand at me.

'I have no quarrel,' he stuttered. 'We do not need to fight.'

I nodded, and leaned against a tree. Finally, when I felt recovered I asked the Soal who he was.

'I am called Kaltan,' he replied.

I picked up Endrod's brainstinger and pointed the weapon at Kaltan.

'Well, Kaltan, you are going to take me to the Soal fleet.'

He hesitated. Then said without expression, 'That's up to you. I want to live, but if you come with me, you will die. They will never let you get to the new humans with the location of the fleet in your possession.'

'Let's go,' I insisted.

We made one diversion. I had made my decision with regard to the women in my life and we called at Tiptihani's home island in the hope that she would have returned there after the revolution had been broken : she was there and I told, not asked, her to accompany me. The rest of the journey in the craft Kaltan had uncovered, apart from a short hop over the sea wall, was by Schooter tube. As soon as I saw where we were headed I realized how slow my brain was. This was the secret of the high ranks, which Endrod had given to my father. This was what he had died for.

The needle towers were the ships.

The towers were metal plated now, and shone steely in the sun. I realized that as soon as the inhabitants got wind of the Martian arrival, the towers would be abandoned. The mudwalkers would be free to step on dry land once more. The fleeing Soal would make for them in the night, once they knew for certain their defences were breached, and on pressing the right switches, allowed a curtain of metal to slide up from beneath the mud where it had been poised for centuries.

The drive and control room would be below the mudline, under a movable flooring. Or perhaps in the nose? I had never been to the top of a needle tower – it had never been possible to go past the sixteenth segment. Yet I had known, somehow, at the time that I was not at the pinnacle of the tower.

'Take me to the Klees of Brytan's ship,' I ordered the unresisting Kaltan.

'He no longer lives. Killed on the night of the invasion.'

'Lintar, his son?'

Kaltan nodded. 'He regained his former position when the Martians came.' Then, 'Your escape is blocked now,' he said grimly. 'We have been seen by the new humans. You became a Soal this day.'

'Quickly then,' I ordered.

We left the chiton and entered the open door of the needle tower.

Once through the locks I surveyed the hostile faces of about a dozen Soal.

'Where is Lintar?' I asked.

A voice spoke to my left and I turned to face my old companion. He was expressionless and waiting. Responsibility was now apparent in his stance and manner.

'We wish to come with you Lintar,' I requested. 'I have no place amongst these aliens that crowd our old planet. This was our birthplace, not theirs, yet they stamp over it like ancient beasts – mindlessly. There are more of them coming – millions they say. This woman,' I indicated my companion, 'and I have no wish to share our world with dinosaurs. We would rather take our chances with the Soal. Kill us or take us! But do not leave us behind alive.'

'Kill you?' his beak opened and closed quickly. 'How could I kill my lifelong companion. But we must go quickly. I will talk to you later. Do not mind the others. They will get used to you once I have spoken with them.'

So we left in a cloud of muck and ooze, spraying everything for hundreds of kilometres with the product of millions of months of elemental toil.

The star shone down on two figures standing by the shore. One cast a long, lean shadow. The other, not quite so long.

'What were they? I was told they were dwellings – rest houses for mud men,' said the Martian.

'What in Weyym's name are you running on about?' said the Earthman. Already there was much animosity between the two races. The Martians had begun to talk of reservations on the continental steppes.

'The ships or towers or whatever they were you fool.'
The answer was delivered in a sullen tone.
'Who's the fool? You could have checked them.'
'We took your word for it.'
'Foolish thing to do. We're ignorant savages.'

A short, red-haired Martian girl lay beside her latest lover and stared up at a star. It was not the same star as that which shone on the foolish Earthman and his arrogant quizzer, for she was in the southern hemisphere, but it was very similar in that it shone whitely and without flickering. She had heard about the starships and she knew what she had lost.

What the Martian hell, she thought. He was never a human anyway. He was a Soal inside a human's skin. She thought this but quietly, without waking her lover, she cried the tears of a woman who was lost.

'Look – beautiful stars,' said the Polynesian girl, not looking up. She was talking to the infant cradled in her arms. It was too small even to focus its eyes on a finger centimetres from its face, let alone a star, light-years out in space, and the husband at the tiller smiled indulgently.

He then looked up himself, searching for the one star he needed to steer by. He was following a *Kaveinga*, going south, to his wife's former island. Now that her mother had gone with the man Cave she felt homesick on her husband's island – and he had no real preference. As long as there were palms and pineapples, and fish to fish, he was as happy as a man can be. Oceania was his home. Several million square kilometres of blue water, studded with green stars.

Once we were on our way we were allowed to release ourselves from the couches. I went to Tiptihani and held her close, as she was afraid. We did not know where we were going, or what we would find once we arrived. It would not take long, for these ships of Lintar's were the old ones, in which they had travelled to Earth, and I knew from Soal history that the last journey was a short one, which it needed to be because there was little edible food on board.

Lintar entered the segment and flicked a switch. The segment lights dimmed and the ceiling darkened, then became freckled with lights. We were staring out into space, looking at its sparkling offerings.

'Which place are we going to?' asked Tiptihani.

Lintar lifted her hand.

'Point to a star,' he said.

THE INCANDESCENT ONES

Fred and Geoffrey Hoyle

Young Peter, a student of Byzantine Art in Moscow University, receives through a cryptic sentence in a lecture a message to buy two books of his choice at a specific hour in the University bookshop. When he opens the package, a third book has been included – a book which sends Peter on a series of adventures leading to the unravelling of a mysterious power source guiding the destinies of planet Earth. His quest is also intimately linked with his father's baffling disappearance.

Once again the Hoyles have succeeded in combining an enjoyable piece of story-telling with scientific speculation of lasting interest.

XANTHE AND THE ROBOTS

Sheila MacLeod

'Xanthe is a member (female) of a research team which is investigating the possibilities of humanoid robots, in a world of chaos and starvation ... Two types of robot have been produced: the Pragmapractors, who do the conventional manual work; and the Philophrenics, who have been programmed to more human levels, to feel affection, to talk, and even construct themselves. The question is: should they be allowed to go further? This is a remarkable story, blending the best of both science fiction and the mainstream novel of character' – *Manchester Evening News*

'Brilliantly realized' – *Time Out*

THE STATUS CIVILIZATION

Robert Sheckley

'Will Barrent is sent to a convict planet for a murder he doesn't remember committing, and finds that unguarded life there is a blackly comic mirror image of Earth: malice through a looking-glass ... A thought-joltingly good read' – Tom Hutchinson in *The Times*

'Superbly demonstrates the full misanthropic joys of the genre ... a *tour de force* of delightful perversity' – Martin Amis in the *Observer*

ROADSIDE PICNIC

Arkady and Boris Strugatsky

The Zone is a part of Canada that has been the scene of a mysterious alien visit. The debris left behind – the equivalent, it is theorized, of the litter humans might scatter at a picnic – is as incomprehensible as they are. Much of it is highly dangerous, but there are some items, such as self-reproducing everlasting batteries, which could revolutionize man's technology. For those who brave the dangers, avoiding official scientific expeditions, the rewards are great. They are the 'stalkers' ...

'The story is carried off with controlled fierceness that doesn't waver for a minute; one can hardly think of a dozen American SF novels written with such command and concision. Please, somebody, *more*' – *Kirkus*

PULSAR 2

An Original Anthology of Science Fiction and Science Futures Edited by George Hay

Sparkling ingredients include new stories by Alan Dean Foster, E. C. Tubb, Robin Douglas, Garry Kilworth, Robert Carter and Rob Holdstock ...

Chris Evans interviews van Vogt, and in an imaginative freewheeling piece Richard Weholt discusses SF in relation to nuclear technology And more ...

MORE WOMEN OF WONDER

Science fiction novelettes by women about women, edited, with an introduction and notes by Pamela Sargent

One of the great appeals of science fiction has always been that it both reflects the present and forecasts the future. For many years, its women characters appeared only in the traditional roles of damsels in distress, wives and mothers, or occasionally tempters. Today women writers are producing some of the best science fiction – with female protagonists.

In this new collection of stories, C. L. Moore, Leigh Brackett, Joanna Russ, Josephine Saxton, Kate Wilhelm, Joan D. Vinge and Ursula K. Le Guin explore feminist themes beyond the frontiers of fact.